When I Surrender

Kendall Ryan is the *New York Times* and *USA Today* bestselling author of contemporary romance novels, including *Hard to Love*, *Unravel Me*, *Resisting Her* and the *Filthy Beautiful Lies* series.

She's a sassy, yet polite Midwestern girl with a deep love of books, and a slight addiction to lipgloss. She lives in Minneapolis with her adorable husband and two baby sons, and enjoys cooking, hiking, being active, and reading. Find out more at www.kendallryanbooks.com

Also by Kendall Ryan

Filthy Beautiful series
Filthy Beautiful Lies
Filthy Beautiful Love
Filthy Beautiful Lust
Filthy Beautiful Forever

Unravel Me series
Unravel Me
Make Me Yours

Love by Design series
Working It
Craving Him
All or Nothing

When I Break series
When I Break
When I Surrender
When We Fall

Hard To Love
Resisting Her
The Impact of You

When I Surrender

Kendall Ryan

HARPER

This novel is entirely a work of fiction.
The names, characters and incidents portrayed in it are the work of the author's imagination. Any resemblance to actual persons, living or dead, events or localities is entirely coincidental.

Harper
An imprint of HarperCollins*Publishers*
1 London Bridge Street
London SE1 9FG

www.harpercollins.co.uk

A Paperback Original 2015
1

A catalogue record for this book is available from the British Library

ISBN: 978-0-00-813396-2

Chapter One

Knox

The girl, whose name I couldn't recall, writhed beneath me on the bed, ready and waiting. My pulse spiked as I watched her tempting curves move in the moonlight.

'Go down on me.' She squirmed, wiggling her hips as if to entice me south.

'I'm not eating your pussy. You're a stripper, baby, I don't know where that thing's been.' It was probably an asshole thing to say, but that shit was the truth.

She let out a short laugh, but didn't disagree.

'Roll over. I want you from behind.' That way I wouldn't have to look into eyes that weren't McKenna's when I sank inside her. The darkness inside me had lain dormant for too long. Because of *her*. It was probably a good thing she figured out I was all wrong for her before I did something bad.

I reached for a condom, knowing that the dual sensations of relief and regret would soon be flooding my system. It was familiar to me, and a feeling I welcomed. Even as I rolled the condom on, I knew this dull ache inside wouldn't be satisfied by the girl in front of me. But this was who I was and I wasn't fighting it anymore. McKenna might have helped me see the light, but she wasn't here now. Just this warm, willing girl who wanted me. Sinking into her slick heat was the only thing I needed to numb my pain. Not to be psychoanalyzed by a girl who would probably never trust me anyhow. I'd lost McKenna anyway, so why was I even thinking about that? The truth was, she was still the only woman I thought about day and night, even when I was about to satisfy my needs with some random hookup.

The pattern was impossible to ignore – I'd lost every woman I cared for, beginning with my mother several years ago. That had been the start of my descent into becoming the man I was now. Thoughts of my mother did nothing to relax me. In fact, I felt on edge and wound tighter than ever.

'What's wrong? What are you waiting for?' The girl shifted to her side and gazed up at me, obviously looking for the same release as me. Blinking several times, I fought to understand what I was seeing – her dark hair and eyes made her resemble my mother. *What the fuck?* I scrambled away from her on my hands and knees.

With my heart hammering against my ribs, I opened my eyes to blackness all around me. I blinked again, struggling to see.

I was in my bed, alone, sweat glistening along my skin. It'd all been a dream. *Thank God.* My room was as dark and empty as my heart. I took a deep, shaky breath and scrubbed my hands over my face while adrenaline pulsed through my veins. I needed to calm the fuck down.

Knowing I wouldn't get back to sleep anytime soon, I climbed from bed and headed downstairs. I downed a glass of cool water and checked on the boys, who were all sleeping soundly, before returning to my own bed. I fell onto the mattress with a thud, my heartbeat still too fast to fully relax.

It'd been a week since I'd seen McKenna – sobbing and hysterical over the thought that I'd slept with Amanda. It still tore me up remembering her like that. I'd done my best to calm her, to try and make her see reason – that I was messed up and it was only a matter of time before I really hurt her – but I hadn't touched that girl. She'd fled the building without a backward glance. She either didn't believe me, didn't care, or both.

I stared up at the ceiling as the minutes ticked past. My mother's death left a cool, empty place inside of me, and McKenna running away only intensified that.

I hated this sick need that followed me into the night. The desperate wanting that tightened my balls against my stomach. I knew only one way to make it go away. I needed to forget, to bury myself deep in distraction and pleasure. I forced my eyes closed and tried to breathe through the craving. Sweat broke out over my skin and my heart sped. *Shit.* I hated this side of myself. Trying to quiet my swirling mind, I thought of McKenna, of her quiet confidence and wholesome beauty. Bad idea. My dick started to rise to attention, liking the new direction of my thoughts. I considered grabbing the bottle of Jack that sat untouched in my nightstand drawer and downing a healthy measure to force my brain into oblivion. Switching tactics, I focused instead on my brothers. I would do anything to protect them from the man I'd become. I had to fight these feelings inside myself.

The fact that I was even questioning all this, trying to calm my raging nerves without sex or alcohol, meant one thing. McKenna had gotten under my skin. And hell if a part of me didn't like it. She was a fascination, someone I wanted to understand. And I felt that way around very few people. I had the boys, and I rarely made time for others. Even friends I'd once been close with no longer counted on my list of priorities. Besides, most were busy being twenty-two years old while I was busy playing dad and sinking deeper and deeper into a hole.

Pulling in a deep breath, I began to relax. I pictured Tucker's uneven grin when he'd sunk that basket straight through the net earlier. I thought about my mother's upcoming birthday and made a mental note to buy flowers and take the boys to her grave. I thought about all the little things I needed to get done this week. Luke's upcoming college placement tests that we needed to register and pay for, Tucker's family tree that we needed to create for his history lesson, and Jaxon… I had no clue what was going on with my eighteen-year-old brother, only that he seemed to be becoming more and more like me. Which made my stomach cramp with fear. I wouldn't wish this life on anyone.

Rolling over and shoving my pillow into place, I released a heavy sigh and closed my eyes, praying for sleep to take me.

Chapter Two

McKenna

I hadn't planned to go on this retreat with Belinda, but given the current state of my life, running away for the weekend sounded like the exact thing I needed. The retreat was for addiction counselors in the Chicago area. There would be panels and lectures over the course of two days. We'd learn about advanced treatment techniques and also take much needed time to rejuvenate with yoga classes and meditation. It sounded a little silly to me and I hadn't wanted to go. I'd planned on staying home and throwing myself into my punishing routine of working and volunteering, but Belinda was my mentor and, well, basically I hated letting people down. So here I was, in the passenger seat of her minivan, watching the miles tick past while unease churned inside of me.

I regretted the way I'd broken down, sobbing, and fled from the group I was supposed to be leading last Saturday. I regretted how close I'd grown to Knox in such a short time, and that he'd been able to break me so easily. Ever since Knox Bauer had first walked into my sex addicts meeting, my life had been in one giant freefall. Despite his baggage, falling for him had been the easy part. Some of my best moments were the quiet ones shared alone with him. The times he'd made himself vulnerable and opened up to me had felt like something. Something real and important. And hanging out with him and his three younger brothers was a nice distraction from the guilt and pain of my everyday life.

But I'd been forced to see the harsh reality of the situation. Knox was a sex addict. Even if he was telling the truth and he hadn't slept with the girl from our group, Amanda, like I'd thought, he still had an addiction. Which meant he was dangerous for me, not someone to give my heart to.

'What's on your mind?' Belinda asked, peering over at me before letting her eyes drift back to the road.

I should have known she'd be perceptive. She was a counselor, trained in reading people and situations, just like me. And I had zero emotional energy left to try and act bubbly and personable, so there was no sense faking it. I'd been sitting here sulking for almost an hour. 'Just some guy troubles,' I admitted.

'Is this about your roommate Brian?' She had a good memory. In a moment of over-sharing I'd once admitted how I didn't think my long time best friend Brian was on the same page with our friends-only status.

'No. But Brian has complicated things a little.' *Or a lot.* He and Knox had gotten into a fist fight because he didn't think Knox was good enough for me. 'It doesn't matter now anyhow, I called things off with the new guy.' I had to. Even though I hadn't known him long, Knox had the ability to turn me inside out and destroy me. And it wouldn't be fair to his brothers for me to parade through their lives and then disappear. Not to mention it'd be unfair to shred the broken fragments of my heart in the process.

'Hmmm,' Belinda purred, squinting as she concentrated on the highway. 'Have you ever given thought to why Brian was so upset?'

'Of course. He didn't like that there was suddenly another man in my life.'

'And why do you think that was?'

I fixed my mouth into a polite smile. I could see what she was doing. My degree was in counseling, too. But the last thing I wanted to talk about was my lonely roommate Brian.

'Have you ever considered that Brian may be the better choice for you?' she pushed on.

'Belinda….' I gave her a mocking look. She needed to cut out the typical therapist questions. Everything about my body language screamed that I didn't want to talk. And no, Brian wasn't the better choice. I hated how everyone saw his rumpled blond hair and blue eyes and thought we'd look great together. He was cute – so what?

She chuckled. 'Sorry. I didn't mean to pry. I can just tell something's bothering you.'

Knox had already stolen my heart, was I really willing to risk my job too by telling Belinda I'd been seeing a man who was supposed to be in treatment? I thought better of it and shook away the thoughts. 'I'll be fine. This weekend away came at just the right time.'

She nodded. 'Let me know if I can help.'

Not unless she could go back in time and tell the old me not to get involved with a man so broken. But even as the thought filtered through my brain, I knew there'd be nothing she could have said that would have made me see reason. I'd been a goner right from the very beginning. His rugged beauty, masculine scent, those dark haunted eyes that spoke of his troubled past – all of it called to me. In his magnetic presence I felt fully alive. And I missed that feeling.

Those first two days were the hardest. I couldn't convince Brian that I was okay, no matter how many times I said it. His worried stare followed me around our shared apartment. Somehow I suspected he knew my foul mood was about Knox, but I didn't want to give him the satisfaction of knowing that was true. I didn't want to hear, 'I told you so.' So I would go into the bathroom and turn on the shower to cry. The scalding hot water would steam up the bathroom and fog over the mirror so I didn't have to see myself lose it. I cried for myself, for Knox, for everything we'd both lost. I cried over my parents like I hadn't in years. I guess feeling brutally alone and lonely would do that to you.

Despite the messed up circumstances surrounding how we met, Knox and I shared a deep connection. I wasn't ready to give that up. But since my heart didn't know what was best for me, my head had to make that decision. I needed to keep my distance. And being two hundred miles away for the weekend was a start.

I checked my phone again. There was a text from Brian telling me to have fun, but nothing else from Knox. After my blowup last weekend, he'd sent one text, '*We should talk*.' That was it. I hadn't responded, afraid I'd run right over there to him again and not be able to walk away this time. He was my addiction and this time away was my treatment.

Meditation was pointless. Every time I closed my eyes, it was Knox's face that I saw. Every time the instructor told us to focus on something that made us happy, I thought about cuddling on the couch with Knox's littlest brother, Tucker. But I trudged through the lectures and seminars, intent on wiping my memory of all those stolen moments.

Chapter Three

Knox

A week had passed without any word from McKenna and I was starting to regret letting her walk away last weekend. At the time I figured she needed to cool down, take some time to process things, but now I saw that she'd been running. Away from me and my messed up pile of baggage just like I knew she'd end up doing eventually.

While she'd been wrong about Amanda, she'd been right about me. Even if I wasn't comfortable with the label, I had a problem with sex. I used girls to escape. I needed the pleasure to numb my feelings of pain and sadness. I just didn't know if I was capable of changing it.

I tucked a box of cereal under one arm and grabbed a gallon of milk before heading into the dining room. 'Come on, Tuck. Breakfast time,' I called to my youngest brother who was stumbling in from the living room sleepy-eyed. I just needed to get the boys on the bus then I could set out on my mission.

There was a line out the door and wrapping around the side of the building when I arrived. I took a chance and headed around to the back, hoping to find another entrance. With only an hour to spare before I had to be at work, I couldn't afford to waste time standing in a line. The heavy steel door at the back of the building was propped open by a large trash can. I was in luck.

I slipped inside, stepping into a huge commercial kitchen. I pulled a white apron over my head from one of the hooks on the wall. Unless I wanted to get thrown out of here before I found her, I needed to look the part. The kitchen bustled with activity – several apron-wearing volunteers were stationed behind a steel countertop, chopping and mixing, and a man with a white chef's hat was cooking something on an eight-burner gas stove. No sign of McKenna, though.

A dark skinned woman stepped in front of me, blocking my path. 'Are you cooking or serving today?' She propped a hand on her ample hip, seemingly annoyed by the sight of me.

'Ah, serving,' I said. Since I didn't see McKenna in the kitchen, I was hoping that meant she was in the dining room.

'Then where are your gloves and hair net?' she questioned, narrowing her eyes.

I glanced around the room and spotted a box of plastic gloves and hairnets on a table behind her. 'Sorry.' Shuffling past her, I grabbed my supplies and headed toward the dining hall. Shoving the net over my hair and slipping on the gloves, I searched for McKenna.

I spotted her several yards away filling little plastic cups of orange juice at a banquet table. She was deep in concentration and she'd yet to notice me. A line of tension creased her forehead and she looked tired. When she hadn't shown up for group on Saturday, I hated thinking it was because I'd driven her away.

She'd once told me that she came to this soup kitchen most mornings to serve breakfast, so I'd taken a chance coming here today. A chance that had paid off. Now I just needed to get her talking to me again. The doors opened and people began lining up with their trays in hand. I stationed myself at the table next to McKenna's. I felt her eyes on me, but rather than glance her way, I picked up the set of tongs and set an apple on each person's tray as they passed me.

'What are you doing?' McKenna hissed over at me.

Picking my head up, I glimpsed over at her, flashing a guilty smile. 'Oh, hey. I'm just volunteering. You?'

Her eyebrows drew together and she let out a huff, obviously not buying my story. She was angry. Good. At least I was getting a reaction. Indifference would have been worse. Anger I could work with.

'Here you go, Mr. Bronson.' Wiping away the scowl meant only for me, McKenna smiled at the older man in front of her, and placed a cup of orange juice in his trembling hands. We were at the end of the line, and by the time they made their way over to us, their plates were loaded with oatmeal, scrambled eggs, and sausage links. It looked pretty damn good for a free breakfast. It smelled good, too. I would have never imagined there were so many people here in line so early for this. Of course McKenna had known, which was why she donated her time and efforts here. A quick glance at my watch told me I only had forty minutes left before I had to leave for my shift managing the hardware store. I needed to speed this process up.

I didn't grovel. I didn't beg, but shit if this girl didn't make me want to drop to my knees and plead for forgiveness. I must be getting soft. An elderly guy pushing a walker approached my table next. One of the staff members was holding his tray for him. 'Apple?' I offered, picking up a fruit with the plastic tongs and holding it out to him.

'With these false teeth?' He smiled, a big gap-toothed grin. 'I better not. I'm not feeling real adventurous today. But thanks for asking.'

'Anytime, man.' I set the apple back down on my table, feeling useless once again. 'I could always go back to the kitchen, see if we have something else. A banana maybe?' I had no idea what they had back in their kitchen, but I was willing to try. This guy was someone's grandfather most likely. I didn't particularly like the idea of him going hungry.

He took my hand and gave it a shake. Misty blue eyes met mine as he grinned at me again. 'Bless you for what you're doing. You're a good person.'

'Trust me, I'm not. But I'm trying.'

'Ah, what the hell. You only live once, hit me with one of those apples.'

I placed a shiny red apple on his tray and felt McKenna watching. Glancing her way, I knew she'd overheard the entire exchange. I'd meant those words. I wasn't a good person. But I wanted to be. For her. 'We need to talk,' I said, low under my breath.

'Not now,' she breathed, her eyes slipping closed. She looked like she was on the verge of tears. I wouldn't push her right now, but I didn't have much time left.

'I have to be at work soon.'

She looked over at me again, confusion marking her features. 'You came here before work?'

She knew it was a big deal that I'd taken the time to come here. Good. 'Got up early, got the guys off to school, and yeah. I came to see you. You didn't return my text. I thought you were ignoring me.'

Drawing a deep, but shaky breath, McKenna continued looking straight ahead. 'Can we just enjoy this?'

I knew volunteering was important to her and I suddenly realized she thought I was interrupting. 'Can we talk later, then?' I asked.

She nodded. 'Okay.'

'McKenna?'

'Yeah?' Pretty blue eyes flashed on mine.

'I didn't sleep with her.'

She set down the cup of juice she was holding with trembling hands. A moment later she disappeared out of the room, treading down a long hallway, and I took off after her.

Shit. She'd agreed to talk later, and yet I kept pushing. But I needed her to believe that. I hadn't laid a hand on that girl. And after hurting her so badly the last time we were together, my own conscience needed clearing.

I heard soft sobs coming from the women's restroom and I pushed open the door and entered, securing the lock behind me. The stall door on the end was closed and I could see her gray tennis shoes beneath the opening. 'McKenna?'

The cries stopped. 'Go away, Knox.'

Fuck. I slumped against the wall, fighting the urge the punch something. 'I just needed to see you, make sure you were okay. The way we left things last time….'

'I'm fine, okay. Or at least I was going to be. Being here is my sanctuary, my escape. But now you've taken that from me, too.'

She was hiding in the damn bathroom stall because of me. I should have felt sorry I'd come, but I didn't. I'd needed to see her with my own eyes or I was going to lose it. 'When you didn't show up Saturday, I kind of freaked out. Are you done leading group?' *Because of me?*

'No, I was at a retreat with counseling seminars all weekend.'

'Can I just tell you one thing?'

She sniffed. 'And then we'll talk about the rest later?'

'Whatever you want.'

'Okay.'

'I never slept with Amanda. Not even close. I have no desire to sleep with her. We exchanged phone numbers because she wanted someone to talk to about raising a baby while recovering from addiction, and I'd told her I have custody of my three brothers. She's freaked out that she has a baby on the way and wanted someone to talk to.' There was a long pause from McKenna. 'Do you believe me?'

'If you weren't with her, then why did you answer that it'd only been one week since your last sexual encounter? Were you with other girls while we were….' A choked little sob escaped her throat.

'Do you want to know why I said that it'd been one week since my last sexual encounter?'

Silence. She thought she didn't want to hear this. But she did.

'When I answered that question, it'd been one week since you'd come to me in the night, let me kiss and touch you. And even without sex, that was the most erotic encounter of my life. Touching you over your panties, knowing you trusted me, making you come… that meant everything to me. It wasn't even about sex. It was about trust. And after that, all other memories of girls I'd been with were wiped from my memory. There was only you. So that's why I said one week. And no, there's been no one else since.'

The bathroom door unlatched, and McKenna stepped out slowly. Her eyes were watery and the tip of her nose was pink. She was still the most beautiful girl in the world. She'd pulled off her hair net and gloves at some point, reminding me that I still had mine on. I smiled weakly at her and pulled off the accessories, dropping them into the nearby wastebasket.

Crossing the room toward me, I opened my arms and McKenna folded herself against my chest. I held her and gently swayed with her in my arms. It'd been a tough week for her. Distress was written all over her features and she felt thin and frail. I wanted to take her home and put her in my bed and never let her go again. Instead I continued lightly rubbing her back, letting her calm down and collect herself. I'd wait as long as it took. I no longer cared about getting to work on time. If she needed me, I wasn't going anywhere.

A few moments later, she lifted her head from my chest and crossed the room to stand in front of the sink, inspecting herself in the mirror.

'You look beautiful,' I murmured. She smirked at her reflection in the mirror. It was the truth. She splashed cool water on her cheeks and I handed her a paper towel. 'You okay?'

She nodded. 'Yeah. I'm okay. Thanks. And I know you have to get to work.'

'Can we still talk later?'

'There's more?' she asked, pushing a chunk of hair behind her ear.

'We need to discuss you and me.'

'There's a you and me?' she breathed.

'You know there is.' My heart thumped steadily in my chest. My relationship with her was the only real thing in my life. Even if it wasn't a romantic relationship, I needed her presence. My brothers did, too. We'd figure the rest out later. 'When are you free?'

'Tomorrow night. I'm attending a fundraiser at the library. It goes until 8:00.'

'Come over after?'

'You'll be a gentleman?' The hint of a smile played on her full lips.

'If you like.'

She exhaled a deep shuddering breath, like she was summoning her courage. 'I'll come.'

The urge to take her in my arms again was overwhelming, but I resisted it. As difficult as it was for me, I needed to learn to deal with shit without falling back on physical touch. 'See you then.'

Chapter Four

McKenna

I took my time getting ready, telling myself I wanted to look nice for the library fundraiser. It was an after-hours event with hor d'oeuvres and wine tasting. I should dress up a little, right? It had nothing to do with seeing Knox after. *Yeah, right.*

I was still reeling with the emotional turmoil stirred up by being near Knox. Getting away last weekend for the retreat was supposed to bring clarity, but all it did was make me miss him more. And then knowing he planned his work day around seeing me at the soup kitchen yesterday had torn down my final wall. Every time I thought I had Knox figured out, he surprised me and pulled me back in. With him, I knew the road was guaranteed to be bumpy, but at last I was moving forward.

I inspected myself in the mirror one final time. My dark hair fell in loose waves down my back and my fitted black pants and silky gray blouse looked simple, but chic. I puckered my lips in the mirror and added a dab of pink lip gloss. *Stop stalling, McKenna.* I grabbed my coat and purse and flipped off my bedroom light.

'You look nice,' Brian said as I entered the living area. The football game was playing in the background. I found it sort of oddly endearing how he'd become a hardcore Chicago sports fan, now cheering for every local team. It was just another way he'd changed his life and habits to support me in this move.

'Thanks.' I smoothed my hands over the fabric of my pants. 'I have this fundraiser thingy at the library tonight.'

'You look like you're going on a date.' His eyes glanced over my curves and came to a stop on my face again. My cheeks heated.

'Nope. Just the library.'

'Maybe I should join you.'

'No!' He couldn't know I was going to Knox's after. I calmed my voice and started again. 'I mean, no, that's not necessary. It'll probably be boring. A few speeches and sign up opportunities for volunteer work in the coming year. Nothing too exciting. Besides, I wouldn't want you to miss the Bears winning their big game.'

'You know I would for you.'

He was too good to me and I was hit with a pang of guilt about lying where I was headed. 'Thanks, but no. You stay, enjoy your game.' I slipped on my coat. If the chill in the fall air was any indication, winter was just around the corner.

'Hey, you wanna do something this weekend?'

'Uh, sure. Sounds great, Bri.' It was probably time we put this awkwardness behind us and forget about his fight with Knox.

The closer I got to Knox's place, the more anxious I became. I was fidgety and distracted all during the fundraiser and watching the clock hadn't helped. The entire evening had dragged by at a snail's pace.

Knox was like a magnet drawing me to him. The pull was primitive and all consuming. And not because I was a fixer, like Brian said, but because our wounded souls found solace in the company of each other. He'd been like a balm to my unseen injuries. And I'd wanted to believe I was his healing balm, too. But I hated that I hadn't been. Despite his little speech in the bathroom, I worried he was still seeking nameless, faceless girls to soothe his aches, which was why I needed to face reality. Sex was his drug of choice. If I'd really meant something to him, he would give all that up, right? I questioned if he could have a relationship that wasn't based on sex. I needed to hear what he had to say tonight, even if it destroyed me in the process.

It was nearly 8:30 by the time I arrived and as I stood waiting on the porch for him to answer the door, I took a few deep breaths of cool air and promised myself that nothing would happen between us. Remembering how his tender kisses and skilled fingers had felt, I inwardly groaned. I needed to be strong.

The door swung open and Knox stood there in jeans, bare feet, and a white T-shirt looking sexy and sinful. 'Change of plans,' he growled.

I followed him inside and shut the door. It was dark and quiet inside. 'Knox?' He continued to the stairs and began climbing them silently. I hurried to keep up with him. 'What's wrong?' His sweet, gentle demeanor from yesterday morning had disappeared, but I wasn't about to let him shut down on me now. We'd come too far for that, hadn't we? We were supposed to talk tonight. 'Knox, what happened?' I asked again as we entered his bedroom.

He opened a dresser drawer, digging through the pile of clothes until he pulled out a long sleeved black T-shirt. 'We're going out. I need to blow off some steam.'

I wondered what had changed his mood and turned him into this closed off version of himself. If he'd slipped up and been with someone, would he tell me? 'Where are we going?'

'To the bar. I need a drink.' He tugged the shirt on over his head and sat down on the bed to put on socks and his boots.

I'd never been to a bar. I was of legal age, but somehow it was just one of those things I hadn't gotten around to yet. The idea of going out with Knox made the skin of the back of my neck tingle pleasantly. 'If I go out with you, will you tell me what happened?'

Dark eyes leapt up to mine as Knox finished lacing his boots. 'Jaxon got in a fight a school. He fucked…um, slept with the quarterback's girlfriend right before the big game.'

'Oh. Did you talk to him, find out why he'd do that?'

'Of course I talked to him. He said the guy was a douche bag and they have gym class together and the guy was always an ass to him. So he wanted revenge. But the team lost their football game because the quarterback was so torn up.'

'And then they fought?'

Knox shook his head. 'No. He got jumped. Because once word got out what Jaxon had done, half the school was pissed at him.'

'And the other half?'

'Thought he was a hero.'

Wow. Talk about high school drama. 'Is he okay?'

'He'll live. He's got some bruises and a fat lip.'

'Is he here?' The nurturer in me wanted to go see if he was okay. Maybe bring him some pain reliever and some ice for the swelling, talk to him about his actions.

Knox nodded. 'Yeah, but they're all in bed early tonight.'

It sounded to me like he'd punished all three boys and sent them to bed early because of Jaxon's mistake, but I kept my mouth shut, unwilling to question him when he was in such a foul mood.

Knox rose from the bed and stalked toward me. 'You ready?'

His plan worried me. Anytime his life got stressful, Knox turned to drinking and sex. I knew they went hand in hand for him. Sudden unease at what the night held in store settled in the pit of my stomach. 'I don't know, Knox. Me? At a bar?'

He shot me a pointed stare. 'What do you do to blow off steam?'

Without giving it a second thought, I rattled off my schedule. 'Monday night I work at the food bank downtown, Tuesday I visit the youth shelter, Wednesdays I've been helping out on a Habitat for Humanity project, Thursdays I go to the Humane Society, and whenever I have time, I serve meals at the soup kitchen. Oh, and Saturday is group.'

He shook his head at me. 'My point exactly. Do you even know how to relax?'

I forced the rigid tension in my shoulders to ease. I could do this. And if I didn't babysit him tonight, who would? 'So where are we going?'

We walked the several blocks to a nearby bar, huddled into our coats the entire time. Once night fell, so did the temperature. Drastically. But once we stepped inside the cozy warmth of the tavern, my spirits lifted. Knox led the way to a booth across from the long bar and we sat down facing each other. It felt intimate and foreign being out with him like this, and I liked it. Knox's eyes remained on mine as I slid out of my coat. He was wearing a dark leather jacket and coupled with the way his long-sleeved tee clung to his broad chest, it made my nipples tighten and rasp against my bra. My entire being took notice of his –on every level– both emotional and physical. It left me staggering for breath.

'So, are we going to talk?' I asked after several tense moments.

'Drinks first.' His eyes cast over to the bar. 'What do you want?'

My gaze followed his. Bottles of liquor were lined up along a glass wall behind the bar, overwhelming me. There were too many choices. 'I- I'm not sure.'

'You've never had a drink before?'

'I've had a drink. But I've never ordered something for myself at a bar before.'

'Beer? Wine? Something fruity? I'll order for you, just tell me what sounds good.'

I chewed on my lower lip. My parents died in a drunk driving accident. I'd never been big on drinking. 'Something fruity I guess. But not too sweet.'

He chuckled at me. 'Got it.'

A few moments later, Knox returned with a pale pink concoction in a tall glass for me, along with a bottle of beer and a shot of something for himself. He pushed the drink toward me and I took a sip from the straw. Mmm. It tasted like lemon-lime soda and cherries with a hint of something tart. Wait a second. 'Is this a Shirley Temple?'

He chuckled and shrugged his shoulders. 'There's alcohol in it.'

'Are you mocking me?' I straightened my shoulders, locking eyes with him.

'Of course not, angel. Drink up.'

I watched as Knox downed the shot in front of him, bringing it to his full lips and draining the glass in an easy swallow.

'Can we talk about what you said at the soup kitchen…about me and you….'

He nodded.

I paused, taking my time. I didn't know if I was really ready to go there with him yet. I decided on a different question that had been plaguing me for some time. 'Knox I know you've told me about your addiction, but will you tell me how it first began? I need to understand. How did you get this way?

'It's second nature. I don't think about it.' His eyes wandered away and he took a long sip of his beer.

'I know. But I'm asking you to. To really examine it. And open up and share with me.' I knew I was asking a lot of him, and I didn't know if he was brave enough.

'I will. In time.'

'What do I have to do for you to tell me?' I chewed on my lip, feeling brave.

He smiled. 'You want inside my head that bad?'

I waited, silent.

'Fine. Take a shot with me.'

I opened my mouth to argue, then snapped it closed again. I could handle one shot. Couldn't I?

This time Knox returned with two shot glasses, each with clear liquor inside. He set one down in front of me and kept the other in his hand. 'This your first shot?' he asked. I nodded. 'Cheers, angel.'

'How do I….' I paused with the shot glass halfway to my lips.

'Tilt your head back. Open your throat. Let it slide down.'

His voice was thick, laced with sexual tension, and my stomach knotted. But I did as he instructed, bringing the glass to my lips and tipping my head back. I felt his eyes on me the entire time, heating up the space between us. The stiff punch of liquor slid down easily, leaving only a slight bitter burn in the back of my throat. I quickly took a sip of my drink to clear away the taste.

'Good girl.' He licked his lips and set his own empty glass down next to mine.

I had a theory that Knox been looking for love and closeness in all the wrong places. His mother died and his father had run off, abandoning the family. And I knew he said he found his peace, if only for a short time, with girl after girl. The feeling never lasted long, though, and so he sought the next girl. I don't think he knew he was stuck in that pattern until I'd come along and forced his eyes open. But I needed to hear Knox say it and connect the dots.

He grabbed his beer and took another swig, his eyebrows knitted together in deep concentration. 'My mom and I were really close. I was a momma's boy and am not afraid to admit it.' He smiled. I remembered the sketches he'd shown me. I knew he loved and missed her deeply. 'When she died, it left this giant hole in me. I began chasing after girls in high school just to feel something. To feel alive. I dated in high school, and slept around a little, but after a while, it just wasn't enough anymore. I needed something more. I started going out to bars and girls were even easier to pick up outside of school. It was simple. I didn't really think about it. And when I was with them, I forgot all about my fucked up life. For a short time anyway. It was a coping mechanism.'

'Didn't that bother you – using them that way? Those were people's daughters.'

'If you think they weren't using me too, you're more naïve than I thought.' He smirked at me, challenging me to disagree.

I'd never thought about it that way, but I supposed he had a valid point. Knox wasn't the type to promise them the moon and stars. He was a take it or leave it kind of guy. And they freely took what he'd offered.

He'd been getting love the only way he knew how – by sleeping with anything with a vagina. It was sad, but on some strange level, I understood. Knox had spent many years feeling unloved and not capable of returning love. But I knew he was capable of more. I saw firsthand how sweet he was with his brothers. He'd stepped up to raise them and set aside his own goals and dreams. And I suspected he wanted to change. He'd been attending my sex addicts meetings for over a month now and hadn't pushed me away, despite my constant questions.

'Still, Knox, you had to know that wasn't right….'

'It's the only thing I know.'

'Then discover something new.' My eyes were pleading with his and I saw the moment my plea registered. His gaze turned hungry as his eyes flicked down to my mouth.

He leaned closer, his eyes soft and probing. 'Meeting you has been interesting for me....'

My heart swelled in my chest and I wanted so badly to hear him continue. But he took a swig of his beer and let his eyes wander out onto the dance floor.

'So assuming you were still…that way, you'd be looking for a girl here tonight?'

'Most likely,' he admitted.

The truth stung, but at least he was honest. We watched in silence as a group of girls, one wearing a tiara and a sash that declared her the *Bride*, shimmied on the dance floor to the beat of hip hop music.

'So if you were here to pick up a girl tonight – who's your type?' I looked on as a blond with large breasts thrust her hips back and forth, too embarrassed to meet Knox's eyes. I wondered if he'd go for someone so obvious about her body and looks. Someone so completely opposite of me.

'You really want me to answer that?' he asked. I nodded, still unable to meet his gaze. 'Look at me,' he commanded.

I did. And his heated stare lit me up from the inside out. I felt my chest and neck flush. I dropped my gaze, sliding my drink toward me and sucking down a big mouthful. 'Yeah, I want to know,' I said, finding my courage. The alcohol flowing through my veins was the likely contributor. When he was like this, so dominant and commanding, my body turned to a pile of mush, ready and waiting for his next command.

Knox's eyes reluctantly left mine and he scanned the dance floor with a bored expression. Not finding anyone of interest, his gaze turned toward the crowded bar. 'I'll be back in a minute,' he said, his eyes not returning to mine.

Unease churned inside me as I watched him cross the room and head down the back hallway alone. What was he doing? Had he already picked out a girl and given her a special wink? I couldn't believe he'd really disappeared and left me sitting here all alone. I sucked down more of my drink as tears blurred my vision.

I hated how I couldn't be what he needed and he chose instead to fulfill his needs without me. I sensed that Knox was developing real feelings, too. So why did he continue on with this charade of hussies? *Because even if he did have feelings for you, McKenna, you're a virgin. You can't satisfy his needs.* That realization sparked something inside me. Rebellion. It made me want to try.

A few moments later, Knox strolled back to the table, his expression unreadable. 'McKenna?' Spotting the unshed tears shimmering in my eyes, he stood immobile in front of the table. 'What happened?'

'You left me.' I pressed my fingertips to my temples, willing the tears away.

He slid into the booth next to me and pulled me close, pressing a kiss to my temple. 'I went to take a piss. You didn't think…?'

I nodded slowly.

'Christ, McKenna. I wouldn't do that. I used the restroom, washed my hands, and came right back to the table.' I suddenly felt foolish for freaking out. He hesitated for several long moments, his jaw clenching in the dim light. 'What do you want from me? You know who I am.'

'Friendship, Knox. I want your friendship.'

'That's it? There's nothing more….' He smiled, crookedly, begging me to disagree.

He was hinting at the burning chemistry between us, brewing just below the surface. My obvious jealous reaction at thinking he'd gone after a girl. He felt this intensity between us and apparently he knew I did, too. I hadn't been hiding my true feelings well enough. He saw it in my lingering gazes, the way I cared for his brothers, and the ways my eyes always went to his while we were in group. There was no point denying it, since I knew eventually he'd see through my game. The truth was I wanted much more than friendship. I wouldn't have taken things physical with him if I hadn't. Something told me he understood that.

I took a deep breath, settling my nerves. 'As for more…yes, I know who you are. You're a man who takes care of his family, who takes on the world for those boys, who works hard and plays harder… but you're also a man on the cusp of change. If you want anything more than friendship with me, then you'll have to show me.'

'Show you what? I told you I don't do love.'

'So change.' I shrugged, flippantly, like it was the simplest thing in the world. Knox said he didn't do love, but he was wrong. He loved his brothers fiercely. He might not have done romantic relationships, but I believed in him, I believed anything was possible, as long as he wanted it bad enough. And selfishly, I wanted to be the one to change his mind about love. He was helping me and some little voice deep inside told me we could do this. It might have been foolish, but when everything else had been stripped away from me, I needed that hope. I would cling to it like a life raft until I was forced to admit he wasn't my savior and I wasn't his.

'What about Brian?' Knox asked, drawing another sip of his beer and signaling the bartender for another.

'What about him?'

'You and him. You ever thought about that? You guys could be good together.'

Was he seriously encouraging my relationship with Brian? After all this? 'First Belinda and now you, really?'

He shrugged. 'Just pointing out your options.'

Frustrated, I pushed a chunk of hair behind my ear. Brian had always been there for me. Would always be there for me. He was sweet and had cute boy next door looks to match. Would it really be the worst thing in the world to see if real feelings could develop between us? Sometimes I wondered about us, but I just didn't feel that way about him, despite what Knox or Belinda saw when they looked at us together. And his encouragement about Brian had the opposite effect, it only made me want to rebel. I took a big gulp from my grown-up Shirley Temple, finishing the drink. 'I'm going to dance.' I didn't dance, but being near him was too much of a roller coaster and I needed a minute to clear my head.

Knox moved aside to let me out of the booth and I headed to the center of the dance floor, ready to lose myself in the crowd. Squeezing my way past the writhing bodies, I found a spot for myself and closed my eyes, letting the thumping rhythm wash over me. Finding the beat, I swayed back and forth to the music. The alcohol had relaxed me enough that I felt totally unconcerned with how I looked to others. I moved and swayed, feeling loose and relaxed as the music took over.

I felt someone approach me from behind, but before my body had the chance to tense, I smelled his unique scent of warm leather and sandalwood and knew it was Knox. He placed both hands on my waist as his chest brushed against my back. A wave of heat crashed over me. He pressed his hips into my bottom and I forgot how to breathe. I spun to face him, needing to see his dark eyes. Was this part of his seduction efforts? He was used to things easily going his way with girls and that fact alone made me want to challenge him a little. He'd just suggested I be with Brian. Did he even really want me?

Knox's hands wandered from my waist to my hips, where his fingertips made contact with bare skin fractures of heat crackled across my abdomen. 'Don't question this.' He leaned down to breathe against my ear.

I danced with him, moving against him, working my hips in what I hoped was an enticing way. Knox's eyes followed my movements and his hands remained planted at my hips.

I'd just told him I wanted his friendship and now I was grinding against him on the dance floor. I knew I was sending mixed signals, but so was he. He'd suggested I be with Brian when all along he'd been possessive about the idea of my male roommate. I should have walked away, gotten some air, but air was the last thing I wanted.

The few disappointing experiences I'd had with a man made me pause. Knox's dominant side gave me hope that he could take control like I craved, allow me to feel like a woman and completely at ease in the bedroom. Was I really ready to walk away from that? I'd spent twenty-one years single, all while fielding questions from nosy friends and relatives about Brian and why I never had a boyfriend. God, I was delusional. Knox wasn't boyfriend material. He wasn't the type of man you gave your heart to. Still, I felt I owed it to myself to find out if he could make me feel this alive on the dance floor, what would it be like in the bedroom? Something in his nature called to mine, and I couldn't turn away.

Chapter Five

Knox

I watched McKenna sway and twist her hips to the beat of the music. She looked beautiful. Pink cheeks, soft curves, and waves of shiny hair flowing around her face. Her eyes were focused on me, and despite asking for my friendship, I knew she wanted more. And somehow I knew it wouldn't be hard to talk her into it. She felt this intensity between us just like I did.

The desire to explore her body, to fuck her until she cried out my name, was getting stronger. And the alcohol clouding my system wasn't helping. The more time I spent with her, the more difficult it became to resist her. And what scared me even more was that the more time I spent with her, the urge to fuck other girls evaporated. There was only McKenna. Her sweet scent, her gentle nature, and her quiet strength to make the world a better place were like a drug to me. I had to have her.

So why was I trying to push her into the arms of another guy? Because I knew it wasn't what she really wanted. She was here in my arms, grinding against *me*. She might have convinced herself that we wouldn't work, so why not let her see that neither would her and Mr. Perfect with his nice car and good job. She needed someone like me – someone fucked up and broken. She just wouldn't let herself believe that yet, so I was giving her a little shove, hoping to expedite the process. And shit, after she said tonight all she wanted from me was friendship – I might have been a little hurt and pissed off and this was my way of rebelling. None of that changed the fact that I had her in my arms and it was my thigh she was currently grinding on. I was taken straight back to that night in my bedroom when McKenna had done this same thing and I'd rubbed her clit until she came. I went instantly hard.

I curled my hands around her waist, pulling her body close to mine. 'You're so fucking sexy.' Her chin dropped down to her chest, and she fiddled with the little silver bracelet on her wrist. She didn't believe that she was sexy. But everything about her was turning me on. The fast inhalations causing her breasts to rise and fall, her flushed skin, the way she completely turned her body over to me… *Fuck.*

It wasn't lost on me that McKenna's interest in me – in my family – was likely because of her need to serve and take care of others. I still didn't know where that need came from. Right now, I didn't care. I needed this girl like I'd never needed anything. 'Let's go,' I growled. She took my hand and let me pull her from the dance floor.

I proceeded to have an internal argument with myself the entire walk home. The right thing to do was to keep my dick in my pants. But when had I ever done the right thing? It wasn't exactly my specialty and ignoring my instincts put me on edge. I wanted her. Badly.

When we reached the house, McKenna quietly toed off her shoes and followed me up the stairs. Once inside my dark bedroom, McKenna paused just inside the doorway, uncertainty written all over her in the pale glow of moonlight. Indecision coursed through me. My own needs would have to take a backseat. I just wanted to make her comfortable.

Wrapping her in my arms from behind, I pressed the brush of a kiss against the bare skin at the back of her neck. 'You okay?' I whispered, letting my chin rest on her shoulder.

'Fine,' she whispered. 'Just…thinking….'

'Overthinking,' I whispered back. 'You tired?'

She nodded, her cheek resting against mine. 'Am I sleeping over?'

'Do you want to?'

She hesitated and I spun her in my arms. As turned on as I'd been on the dance floor, I wanted her to see that she could trust me to go slow. She'd once requested that I be a gentleman with her and I wouldn't betray that trust. She'd done too much for me, taken a leap of faith on even being here and I couldn't fuck this up. Not for me and McKenna and not for my brothers either.

Brilliant sapphire eyes looked up into mine, so trusting and full of hope. She gave a tight nod. Even if she knew she shouldn't want this with someone like me – she did. That was all the reassurance I needed. I wouldn't lure her into my world or force anything on her. The fact that she was choosing to be here meant everything. She knew my fucked up past, and still she was here.

I placed a soft kiss on her forehead and gathered up some pajamas for her. A pair of a sweatpants and an oversized T-shirt I knew would be huge on her. 'For you.' I left the clothes in her hands and headed into the bathroom to give her some privacy. After brushing my teeth and waiting for McKenna to do the same, we crawled into bed together.

In the dim light from the moon and street lamps outside, only the faint outline of McKenna's curves were visible under the sheets. 'Are you warm enough?' It didn't escape my notice that she'd forgone the sweatpants, dressing only in the T-shirt I'd left for her.

She nodded. 'I'm perfect.'

'I agree.'

She chuckled in the darkness. 'That's not what I meant.'

'I know. But it's the truth. Sometimes I don't even know why you're here with me. Why you've never judged me the way others do.'

'I'm no one to pass judgment,' she said sadly.

She was the best, the most pure and selfless person I knew. How could she possibly think that about herself? Maybe it was time to learn about the inner demons that plagued her. 'Will you tell me about your parents? How you lost them?' She stayed quiet. 'You know so much about me and my past, and I want you to know that you can open up to me too, but only when you're ready. I won't force you.'

She nodded. 'No, it's okay. It's time you knew.' She watched my eyes in the dim light as if deciding if she could trust me with the secret that burdened her. 'When I was seventeen my parents died in a car accident. A drunk driver broadsided them on their way to church.'

I found her hands under the blanket and laced my fingers with hers. 'I'm sorry.'

The shimmering hint of tears in her eyes made my heart clench. 'The worst part about it was knowing that it never should have happened. I fought with my mom that morning – I refused to go with them and I was the reason they got on the road late. It was my fault. And the last words I spoke to them were cruel and hurtful. I can never take that back, you know?'

I nodded. I knew about the finality of death and how it caused regrets and what-ifs to creep inside your brain and refuse to leave. 'McKenna.' I squeezed her tiny hands in mine. 'That accident wasn't your fault.' She blinked several times, trying to fight off the tears. It was the damn drunk driver, she had to know that. Seeing McKenna's pain made me feel guiltier than ever about my own drunk driving arrest. But without that wake up call, I doubted I would have ever met her.

'If I'd just been a good daughter that morning, put my own wants aside and gone with them….' A broken cry escaped her throat. 'They'd still be here.'

'Have you heard of survivor's guilt, McKenna?'

'Knox, don't,' she warned.

'It wasn't your fault.' I wish I had better words to say to soothe her pain, but I knew nothing ever would. It wasn't fair how she'd lost her parents. They hadn't deserved what happened to them, any more than my mom had deserved the cancer that took her. Instead, I pulled her closer, into the warmth of my body, and held her next to me and let her cry. Her body shook with silent sobs while I held her, wishing there was something I could do. I rubbed her back and let her soak my shirt with tears and whispered to her that it would be okay. Even if whispered softly and meant to soothe, my words were hollow. I knew from experience that a loss that great wasn't something that ever fully healed. The best I could do was hold her and be there for her. Death and loss made no sense. There wasn't any explaining it or rationalizing it. An accident like that wasn't logical, and neither was McKenna's view on her role. She did nothing to cause their deaths. And I hoped in time I could help her to see that.

After what seemed like close to an hour, her sobs finally quieted and I continued to hold her until the little rasping hiccups stopped, too. She moved from the spot where she'd burrowed in against my neck. 'I'm sorry,' she whispered, and attempted to move back to her side of the bed.

My arms closed around her, keeping her close. 'Never apologize for that. I'm here. And I know what it feels like to lose your parents.'

She nodded. 'Thank you for listening and for holding me….'

'Shh. No need to thank me.'

'Knox?'

'Yeah?'

'This, us what does it mean?'

'What do you want it to mean?'

'More,' she admitted softly.

I had no idea what more meant to her, but I could only assume it involved me fully opening myself up to this process. 'I like you, McKenna. You have to know I'm not like this with anyone but you.'

'I like you too, but this isn't going to be like one of your other relationships.'

'So what do we do?' I traced her cheek and watched her eyes. She would have to take the lead, because I was at a total fucking loss for how to have a real relationship.

'I guess we see where this takes us.'

'I've never had anything like this, how do you know I'm not going to mess it up?'

'Because you're a good man, Knox.'

I pressed a kiss to her lips, surprising her. I hadn't meant the kiss as anything sexual, just a comforting endearment to show her I cared. But McKenna lifted her lips to mine and kissed me back. Her mouth was warm and soft and a jolt of pleasure shot straight to my dick. Now was not the time to get hard. McKenna's body was nestled in against mine, just the thin layer of her T-shirt and my gym shorts separating the heat of her body from mine. She tossed her top leg over my hip and pressed herself closer, no doubt feeling every hard inch of me. I wanted her, but not like this.

McKenna craved physical touch, but in a much different way than I did. She was seeking something real – a connection, something permanent. I never thought I'd be the one to offer her those things, but seeing how brave she was, how open she was with her needs, made me question everything. I wanted to be what she needed. I just didn't know how and was pretty certain I'd find a way to fuck it up. Hurting her was out of the question. She'd been through too much already.

We kissed for several long minutes, our tongues moving together, her breathing becoming ragged, and her lower half pressing clumsily into mine as though she was seeking something.

I hadn't wanted to push things between us tonight, but hell, she'd just broken down and told me she felt responsible for her parents' deaths. If there was ever a time she needed the distraction of pleasure, it was now. I knew that better than anyone.

'Knox....' she breathed, pressing her hips to mine.

I didn't respond, my lips moving to her neck to taste her and breathe in her sweet scent. Her hands scrambled along my abs until they reached the waistband of my shorts. I caught her roaming hands and moved them away just before they dipped inside. We'd just agreed to take the first steps toward a relationship and I didn't want her to think that had anything to do with sex. I wanted her, of course I did, but I wanted more, too.

Sex wasn't the way to show her how I felt about her. That meant nothing to me. But being near her kissing her, cooking for her, letting her sleep over in my bed. Those were the ways I told her how I felt about her. Only now as her fingers curled into my hair and her lips hovered above mine, I didn't think she got that. She wanted the physical, too. And it was killing me. Literally killing me not to take her and push her knees apart and sink into her slowly.

She let out a frustrated groan and rubbed her pelvis against mine. Even if I didn't want her to feel pressured to go further than she wanted, I wouldn't leave her in this state. Trailing my hand from her hip down to her pubic bone, my fingers brushed against her panties. The damp fabric clung to her skin. 'Right here?' She whimpered softly. 'Is this where you need me?' She pushed her hips closer, begging me silently. Lifting her panties aside, I pressed my fingertip against her firm little clit and she let out a ragged moan. Something told me I knew her body better than she did herself, and I liked hearing the responses I provoked from her. I liked knowing

I was the one responsible for her pleasure. The one taking her over the edge. It did insane things to me. Even without touching me, she got me rock hard and aching. Half of me worried we should stop – we'd both been drinking – but none of me wanted to.

Removing my hand from her panties, I pressed a kiss to her parted lips and met her eyes. 'Angel?' Disappointment flooded her pretty eyes. 'How drunk are you?' She'd only had one drink plus the shot I'd made her try, but still, something told me she was unaccustomed to drinking.

She hesitated for a moment, blinking up at me. 'Not drunk,' she breathed. 'Don't stop.' Her mouth crashed against mine in a hungry kiss and I was done questioning this.

Restraint urged me to keep her panties on but I couldn't help lifting the baggy T-shirt she wore and kissing all over her breasts. Using both hands, I pressed her tits together and placed damp sucking kisses all over the rounded flesh, using my tongue to lick each taut peak until she was restless and moaning out my name. She smelled lightly of soap and fresh washed laundry and tasted even better. I was desperate to taste her all over and feel her warm soft skin against mine.

Creaking floorboards signaled that we weren't alone just as I heard my name. 'Knox?'

I tossed the blankets over McKenna to cover her naked chest and jumped up. 'Tucker? What's wrong?'

'My tummy hurts,' he groaned.

'Okay, buddy. Come on.' I led him into the bathroom, my heart pounding out of control. As soon as the toilet was in view, Tucker lurched over it and got sick. I stayed with him in the bathroom, sitting on the tile floor, just in case he got sick again.

A few minutes later, McKenna tapped on the bathroom door. I didn't know if she'd wanted to hide the fact she was staying overnight, but she stuck her head inside the door to see if Tucker was okay. 'You need anything? A glass of water, maybe?'

I nodded. 'Sure, that'd be great.'

After a few minutes more, Tucker rinsed his mouth and crawled into my bed between me and McKenna. By that point it was nearly three in the morning and we were all exhausted. Tucker had insisted she stay and held her hand as he fell back asleep. I caught McKenna's eyes as she lay on the far side of the bed, a sick little boy sprawled between us, and as I watched her in the dim light, she seemed to understand that this was my life. Her eyes on mine and the small smile on her lips was her silent acknowledgement that she accepted each part. From my broken past to my responsibilities with my brothers. McKenna's constant presence here showed me that she could handle not only the fucked up side of me, but also my role as a brother and a parent. It was a huge feeling of relief. Realizing I wasn't alone for the first time in a long time, I feel into a peaceful sleep.

Chapter Six

McKenna

I had sent a quick text to Brian to let him know I wouldn't be home last night. And to my surprise, he hadn't replied. My phone had stayed eerily silent all night. A sinking feeling formed in the pit of my stomach.

After getting Tucker settled in his own bed with some dry toast and soda, Knox and I ventured to the kitchen where Knox set a pot of coffee to brew. I was working at the teen shelter today, but didn't go in until mid-morning, and Knox, with a sick little boy home from school today, was taking the day off to look after him.

Sitting down at the breakfast table, I watched him work. He seemed completely at ease in the kitchen, and for a guy as big and strong as Knox, it was a bit of an anomaly. One I very much liked. His domestic nature, despite being a rugged bad-boy, was just another thing I loved about him.

Luke and Jaxon entered the kitchen and gave me only a brief strange look when they saw me and realized that I must have spent the night. 'Hey, McKenna.' Luke smiled.

'Hey, Luke.'

Jaxon grabbed an apple from the kitchen counter and began slicing it into chunks while simultaneously sizing me up.

'Fuck!' he cursed, dropping the knife and holding his finger up to inspect.

I jumped from my seat and crossed the room to where Jaxon stood. 'Did you cut yourself?'

He shrugged, turning on the faucet to rinse his hand under cool water. 'It's nothing.'

'At least let me have a look.' I took his hand, all but forcing him to let me see. These boys were so brave, so independent, that they didn't want to have to rely on anyone for anything. They'd been hurt so badly losing their parents. They were afraid to need anyone. The slice through the pad of his index finger wasn't deep, but was bleeding pretty steadily. 'I think I can bandage this up pretty quick, it doesn't look too bad.'

'Nah, I'm okay. Luke, hit me with that paper towel.'

'Man-daid?' Luke asked, tossing a roll of paper towel across the kitchen to Jaxon.

Jaxon nodded and began wrapping several sheets around his bloodied finger.

'Man-daid?' I asked, watching their exchange.

'Yeah, like a Band-Aid, but for real men. Paper towel and duct tape.' Luke smiled, tossing Jaxon a roll of duct tape from a nearby drawer.

Jaxon used the tape to secure the paper towel in place. 'See?' He held up the digit. 'All good.'

I shook my head, giggling at their inventiveness. 'What about your breakfast?' I asked, looking over at the discarded chunks of apple on the counter.

Jaxon shrugged. 'I'll grab something later.'

'Have a good day at school, boys.'

Knox met me in the kitchen where I was tidying up after the boys.

He scooped me up in his arms, wrapping me tightly in a hug. 'You don't have to do that.'

'It's not a problem.' I liked helping, feeling useful like this.

'About last night.' His hand closed over mine, stopping me from wiping down the counter so I met his eyes. 'Thank you for telling me about your parents.'

I nodded. I hadn't wanted to tell him – not because I was set on keeping my past hidden, no, he'd been too open with me to do that. But because I knew he'd look at me differently once he knew. I'd seen it before – once people found out, their looks changed to ones of pity, of sadness. I couldn't stand the thought of Knox looking at me like that. But instead he'd just pulled me close and let me cry big soggy tears that rolled down my cheeks and stained his T-shirt. It had been exactly what I needed.

'Let me check on Tucker one more time and then I'll drive you home.'

'Okay.' I followed him up the stairs, wanting to say goodbye to Tucker myself.

We found him curled on his side, the trash can Knox had set next to his bed thankfully still empty.

'How ya feeling, buddy?' Knox sat down on the edge of his bed, handing him a stuffed teddy bear that had fallen to the floor.

Tucker wrapped his arms around the bear and closed his eyes. 'The same. Tummy still hurts.'

Knox pulled the blankets up higher around Tucker's shoulders. 'I've got to take McKenna home and then I'll be right back. You need me to get you anything before we go?'

Tucker's eyes latched onto mine. He was like a mini-version of Knox, and even at eight years old, it was easy to see that he'd grow into a very handsome man, just like his older brothers. Seeing them together made my chest feel tight. Knox was so sweet, so gentle, and watching him care for his brother was the most wonderful sight. He was beautiful to me in that moment. It took me a second to realize Tucker was asking about me.

'Why does McKenna have to leave?' he asked, his features painted in confusion.

'She has to go to work today,' Knox explained.

'But you don't, right?'

Knox shook his head. 'I took the day off. I'm staying home with you today. We can watch a movie later if you want.'

I bent down and placed my hand on Tucker's forehead, checking for a temperature. He didn't seem overly warm. 'I promise I'll come back and check on you. Feel better, okay?'

He nodded, fixing on a brave face. 'Bye, Kenna.'

'Nikki's going to come over while I'm gone. Just in case, all right, buddy?'

Tucker nodded bravely.

Knox led the way downstairs and we dressed ourselves in coats and shoes, waiting by the front door for his neighbor Nikki.

Knox leaned closer, tucking stray strands of hair behind my ears. 'I'm sorry we got interrupted last night. Maybe we can finish our conversation tonight?'

I wondered which part he was sorry got interrupted – our intimate moment or the conversation about my parents? I merely nodded my agreement. Moments later, his young neighbor Nikki let herself in the front door, her baby daughter Bailee balanced on her hip. The baby looked just like her mom – both were pretty with blonde ringlets and big blue eyes. I wasn't sure why, but I hadn't realized his neighbor was gorgeous. She eyed me carefully while Knox took the baby so she could remove her jacket.

'Hi. I'm Nikki.' She offered me her hand.

'McKenna. It's nice to meet you. Your daughter's beautiful.'

She took the little girl back from Knox. 'Thanks.'

I could tell there was something she didn't like about seeing me here with Knox. She probably wasn't used to seeing women here in his home, especially in the morning hours, and I briefly wondered if they'd ever had a fling.

'Tucker's upstairs in bed,' Knox said. 'I'd just stay down here if I were you. Keep both of you away from the germs.'

Nikki nodded. 'I will.'

She crossed the room, sat Bailee down on the rug in the living room, and dumped a nearby basket of toys out in front of her, then planted herself on the couch with the TV remote. The twinge of jealously brewing inside me was unexpected. I knew Knox's past and worked hard to not let it get to me, but something about seeing this girl in his home, somewhere she was obviously quite comfortable, set me off. I pushed it from my mind as Knox led the way out to his Jeep.

The flu progressed from Tucker to Luke to Jaxon and I feared Knox was next, despite his insistence that he felt fine. He'd been taking care of everyone all week; surely he'd exposed himself to the sickness. I knew I was supposed to hang out with Brian that weekend, but Knox hadn't sounded well on the phone, so I'd put my date with Brian off, promising to make it up to him, and decided to go over and check on the guys once more.

The house was quiet. Too quiet. I suspected the boys were home, but they were either napping or doing quiet activities in their rooms. I climbed the stairs to the third floor and lightly tapped on Knox's bedroom door. Not waiting for an answer, I pushed the door open and stepped inside. The blinds were drawn, and the room was quiet, cool and dim. Knox was stretched out across his bed, his big frame limp against the mattress. I didn't even have to ask him if he was sick. It was obvious.

'You shouldn't be here,' he said, sitting up in bed once he saw me. He looked miserable, and I'd guess it was a combination of a few things – lack of sleep being the main contributor. He lifted to his elbow to watch me cross the room. The sheets were strewn haphazardly around him and he was in a pair of loose-fitting gray knit pants and a white T-shirt. His feet were bare and his hair stuck up in several directions. 'We're going to get you sick.'

'Hush.' I sat down beside him and brushed his hair back off his forehead. He felt warm and his cheeks were flushed. I might be in a house filled with germs, but that wasn't even hitting my radar. 'I'm here and I'm staying. You can't do all this on your own, despite thinking you're Superman.'

He chuckled, dryly, his throat obviously raw. 'I don't think that.'

I met his eyes. 'You act like it sometimes. Working hard, raising your brothers, trying to right your wrongs. You're pretty amazing, you know that?' Something about seeing him this sick and miserable made me all sentimental.

'You think that, but it's not true,' he said. I didn't argue, didn't want him to waste his energy debating his point. I knew he was amazing, despite what he thought. I just continued softly brushing back his hair, gazing down at him with reverence. 'You've always thought that, haven't you?' he continued. 'You always believed in me. Even before I believed in myself.'

Of course I did. I was a counselor; I believed people could change, right down to my very being. I had to believe it. It needed to be true if I was ever going to be good enough to outdo the wrong that caused me to lose my parents. Or maybe I just wanted to believe that Knox could change because I'd felt such a pull to him right from the beginning. I'd wanted a little piece of this troubled man, even though it scared me. I needed him to be okay. So did his brothers. 'Just rest. I'm going to go clean up a bit and run to the grocery store.'

He smiled weakly up at me. 'Thank you. There's some money in my top drawer.' He looked over at his dresser in the corner.

He worked hard for his money, but I knew he wasn't any better off than me. If I could help out a little, I would. And there was enough in my bank account this week. I could afford bread and milk and basics for the boys. 'Anything in particular sound good?'

He made a grimace, like food sounded awful. 'Maybe just some soda.'

'You got it.' And perhaps some chicken noodle soup for once they all started feeling better. It was just what my mom would have made if I were sick. I'd get a big pot bubbling on the stove just in case. Fill the house with that yummy aroma in the hopes that would lift their spirits.

I headed downstairs and found Luke and Jaxon on the couch playing the least spirited game of Xbox I'd ever seen. They still looked glassy-eyed and pale, but they were out of bed and apparently well enough to sit and play, but not enough to engage in their usual banter and trash talking. 'You guys feeling better?' I asked, slipping on my coat and shoes.

'Well enough to not be hugging the toilet anymore.' Jaxon smirked.

'That's a good thing.' I winked. 'I'm headed to the store and I'm gonna make some chicken noodle soup later, it'll be ready whenever you feel up for eating.'

'Thanks, Kenna,' they both chimed in.

I would tackle the dishes and bathrooms when I returned. This house was in need of some serious TLC. After a week of four sick boys with no one cleaning up – it looked and smelled the part.

'McKenna?' Luke asked, glancing up from his game.

I paused, turning to face him. 'Yeah?'

'Thanks for making our house feel like a home.' He flashed a perfectly straight white smile at me and my heart melted a tiny bit in my chest. Without a family of my own anymore, I'd been unwittingly making myself part of theirs.

*

When I got home from Knox's place, I was exhausted. I felt like I hadn't slept in a week. I wanted nothing more than to crawl into bed and wrap myself up in the blankets, but first I wanted a nice hot shower. Brian wasn't home, thankfully, so I didn't have to field any questions about where I'd been all day. I knew he wasn't happy about me cancelling our plans to go and see Knox.

Under the steaming spray of water, I washed myself thoroughly, scrubbing away any lingering germs, though I'd been careful at Knox's, washing my hands and disinfecting everything I'd touched over there. Drying myself with an oversized towel, I padded into my bedroom and dressed in pajamas. I didn't care that it was only late afternoon. I felt like going to bed.

Crawling under the covers, I was asleep as soon as my head touched the pillow.

Chapter Seven

Knox

When my texts and phone calls to McKenna went unanswered, I decided to drive over to her apartment to see for myself what was going on. Just as I suspected, she'd come down with the flu. After an unpleasant exchange with Brian, I found her in her bed, curled into a tight little ball.

'McKenna?' I whispered.

Her eyes opened slowly, taking several moments to focus on mine. 'Knox?'

'You caught it, didn't you?' I smiled down at her, brushing her hair back from her face.

'Uh huh,' she nodded.

I knew there'd been no way she could have hung around me and the boys, as sick as we all were for four days straight, and not catch this nasty flu. Something tugged inside my chest seeing her so pale and listless. I wished there was something I could do, but unfortunately I knew this thing had to run its course. 'Can I get you anything?'

She pulled the blankets up higher toward her chin. 'I'm cold. Maybe an extra blanket.' She tipped her chin toward the chair in the corner where a fluffy throw blanket was folded.

I arranged the blanket over her and then crawled into bed beside her. 'Here.' I opened my arms. 'I'll warm you up.'

She snuggled into my chest. 'Mmm. My own personal space heater.'

McKenna dozed in and out of sleep while I lay there holding her. She stopped shivering after about ten minutes and soon her skin was growing damp with perspiration.

Now that my strength had returned and all the boys were healthy again, I'd returned to work. But if need be, I would stay here and care for McKenna, just like she'd done for us.

After a brief knock, Brian pushed open the door. Shooting him a scowl, I wondered if he invaded McKenna's privacy like this often. *Dickhead*. 'Need something?' I asked. McKenna's eyelids fluttered, but she remained curled against my side.

'I'd prefer the door to stay open if you're going to be in her room with her.'

Was he fucking serious? 'Are you her father?'

Opening her eyes, McKenna looked up at me and frowned. My choice of words hit me at that exact moment. *Fuck*. 'I'm sorry. I'll be right back.'

I climbed from her bed and met Brian in the hallway, softly closing the bedroom door behind me. 'What's your problem with me? Or is it with any man being with her that isn't you?'

'McKenna may trust you, but I don't. And I certainly don't trust you alone in a bed with her.'

'She's sick. Do you really think I'm going to try something?'

He shrugged. 'I don't know how you work – what you're capable of.'

'I have issues, I'll be the first to admit it, but I'm not a fucking rapist. Christ.' I shuddered. It made me wonder what McKenna had told him about me. Did he actually think I'd make her do anything she wasn't ready for? The truth was, McKenna had been the one driving the physical aspects of our relationship this entire time. Not that I'd give good old Brian the satisfaction of knowing that.

'She hasn't told you, has she?' Brian smirked.

'Told me what?'

'McKenna's still a virgin. At least I'm pretty sure she is.'

All the air was ripped from my lungs. McKenna was untouched? That piece of information made me both deliriously happy and pissed off. How could she not have told me? What if I'd let things go too far the other night? 'That's her business,' I said, recovering.

Brian narrowed his eyes. If he wanted to believe I was the bad guy, that I was dangerous for her – too fucking bad. McKenna brought out new sides in me, made me feel things I'd never felt before. And I wouldn't hurt her, would never force her. He could think whatever he wanted to about me. I had zero problem knocking him on his ass again if the occasion called for it. And the way my blood was currently coursing through my veins, stirring up anger and resentment inside me, I wondered if now was that occasion. Instead, I took a deep breath and forced myself to calm down. 'If we're through here, I have a sick girl in there to take care of.' I headed into her room and closed the door behind me, signaling that she was mine to care for, not his.

Seeing her lying in bed again, there were a million things I wanted to ask her about. Brian had just dropped a huge fucking bombshell on me and I wanted to ask McKenna if it were true. If she was a virgin, we were on two totally different wave-lengths. What could she be thinking about wanting to enter into a relationship with me? Our conversations came roaring back me. The way she angled her hips to mine the other night, seeking, wanting… I couldn't be expected to control myself and go slow like she needed when she did shit like that.

I sat down on the edge of her bed and let out a heavy sigh.

'What's wrong?' she croaked, opening her eyes.

'Nothing, angel. Just rest, okay?'

She nodded and let her eyes slip closed again. We needed to discuss this, but the conversation would have to wait. One, because

I had no fucking idea what I was doing, and two, because first she needed time to heal.

I pressed a kiss to her forehead and left moments later, reeling from the realization that for once, I was totally and completely out of my element with a girl.

Chapter Eight

McKenna

Monday morning I was finally well enough to get out of bed. I showered and changed into fresh clothes and then ventured out into the living room. Brian sat on the couch with his back toward me, essentially ignoring me. He was dressed and ready for work, but sat motionless with a mug of coffee. I grabbed a soda from the fridge and sat down next to him, wondering what I'd done wrong this time.

'You feeling better?' he asked, his eyes still glued to the commercial playing on the TV.

'Yeah. Sorry, the last few days are a complete blur.' I opened the can of soda and took a small sip, the sugar and fizz tasting delicious after having nothing in the belly for so long.

'We were supposed to hang out this weekend.'

So that's what this was about. Brian was giving me the cold shoulder because I'd had to cancel our plans. Did he really think I purposefully chose being chained to the toilet over hanging out with him? 'Brian, I got sick.'

'You spent all week working hard and then taking care of him.' He shot me an exasperated look. 'What did you expect to happen?'

I shrugged. When he put it like that, I couldn't argue. His anger was misplaced, but I supposed I had exposed myself to the flu.

'It's fine.' He turned to fully face me. 'It helps me see where I fall on your list of priorities. Dead fucking last.'

Seeing how let down he really was made my heart ache for him. Brian always put me first – always. And he was right. He often ranked last on my to do list. Mainly because I knew he would always be there. My job and my volunteer work came first and Knox and his family were a close second. They were the only things that made me feel whole. Yet sitting here, facing him and looking into his sad blue eyes, I felt guilty. Not because I'd gotten sick and missed our weekend plans, but because I'd never feel the way about him that he did for me.

He'd changed his whole life for me. He moved away from his family and friends, he worked long hours at a tough Chicago accounting firm rather than the simple small town firm he probably would've ended up at had he stayed in Indiana. All because of me. And weighing on me most of all was the fact he didn't date. Like he was waiting for me to see him in a different light – waiting for me to be ready. I just wanted him to move on with his life so I could, too.

Knowing he didn't support my relationship with Knox was hard. Brian had always been there to cheer me on through everything in life. He celebrated my small victories and praised my every accomplishment. This chance at something real felt like the biggest thing that had ever happened to me, and Brian didn't support it.

I took my soda back to my bedroom, feeling the need to withdraw into myself once again.

Sitting on my bed, I decided to call Belinda, feeling guilty for missing the last two Saturday group sessions – one because of the retreat, and this weekend's because I was sick.

Belinda disregarded my apology completely. 'Things come up, McKenna. And you were under the weather. No need to apologize.'

'Well, I'll definitely be there next Saturday and please let me know if there's anything I can do in the meantime.'

'Perhaps there is something you could do. Amanda reached out to me on Friday….'

She explained that Amanda had yet to have any prenatal care and didn't have a vehicle to take herself to the doctor.

'Well, I'd be happy to take her, but I don't have a car, either.'

'Hmm. That is a problem.'

'You know what? It's not a problem. I can either borrow my roommate's car or take the bus with her. Maybe just having someone reach out and offer to help will be enough. That way she doesn't have to navigate going to the doctor alone.'

'I think that would help a lot. Very thoughtful of you, McKenna. Thank you.'

'It's not a problem.' It would give me something to do today, since I wasn't due to work at the teen shelter today. Though there was no way I would ask to borrow Brian's car. Not to mention he needed it to get to work. Hopefully Amanda would be okay with taking the bus.

Belinda took care of the details – contacting Amanda and arranging a time for us to meet up at her apartment. I got myself showered and dressed for the day and headed out to wait for the bus.

Amanda lived in a rundown apartment that she shared with three other girls. It didn't look like anyplace to raise a baby, but we'd hurdle one obstacle at a time. The first step was getting her well and making sure her baby was healthy.

'Thanks for doing this today.' Amanda smiled at me as she buttoned her coat.

'It's really no problem. I didn't have anything going on today anyway.'

She paused at the door, hesitating. 'Was everything okay…the last group meeting you ran out of there pretty abruptly, and then haven't been back….'

I smiled at her reassuringly. 'Everything's fine. It was just a slight misunderstanding….' I left it at that. I had to protect what Knox and I had.

'Fair enough.' She nodded, clearly not one to pry.

Amanda, having moved here from southern Illinois, wasn't familiar with the city bus system. So while we rode, I showed her how to read the bus map and explained what the letters and numbers meant so she could learn to navigate the routes. To get to the free clinic downtown from where she lived, it required us to change bus lines twice, and I knew if she could master this, she could get herself anywhere.

'How have you been feeling?' I asked as we watched the traffic pass. Stealing another glance, I noticed her belly now protruded in a nice round bump.

'Actually, I've been having some morning sickness. But other than that, fine, I guess.'

We rode the rest of the way in silence. I found myself at a loss for what to talk with her about. I knew about her issues with love and sex addiction from Belinda, but since she didn't seem to be in a talkative mood, I wasn't going to press her. She likely had a lot on her mind – with a baby growing inside her, no job, no car, and little support.

When we arrived at the clinic, we signed in and sat down in the waiting room. There were several other girls with pregnant bellies waiting in the chairs around us and a few who were most likely here for testing or birth control. Amanda flipped absently through a parenting magazine, not seeming to absorb a single word for how quickly she was turning the pages.

'There's something I feel kind of weird about and I should probably just tell you,' she blurted after several minutes.

'What is it?'

'I, um, came onto Knox.'

My eyes widened. 'What? When?' I fought to control my voice. I couldn't go sounding like a jealous girlfriend right now. As hard as it was, I needed to be objective and professional. Amanda was opening up to me as part of her own treatment.

'In a moment of weakness…it was stupid, I know. He'd given me his phone number and I knew I supposed to use it to call him about recovery and kid-related questions, but one night I was sitting around feeling lonely and sorry for myself and I called him up and asked if he wanted to hang out and have a little grown up fun.'

I nearly choked getting my next words out. 'And did he?' If he'd lied to me about hooking up Amanda, so help me God, I'd lose it. I wasn't a violent person, but the wrath I'd rain down on him would rival the apocalypse.

She chewed on her lip. 'No, he said he was trying to be done with random hookups and made it sound there was someone special in his life.'

Wow. I knew I should respond, but I was rendered speechless.

'You're not mad, are you?'

It took me almost a full minute to realize she wasn't asking because she knew that Knox were sort of together, she was asking because she was supposed to be in recovery. My twisted emotions were going to blow this whole thing if I wasn't careful. 'No, I'm not mad. I won't ever be mad for you opening up and sharing with me.' I took her hand. 'I'm actually proud of you, Amanda. You're growing. You might have slipped up a little, but you recognized that your actions were wrong.' Her confession to me proved that. I released her hand and a smile blossomed across her mouth.

Amanda turned back to her magazine and tore out a coupon for baby formula, stuffing it into her purse. I decided then and there that I liked her. I was glad Belinda had asked me to help. Amanda was actually a sweet girl underneath her layers of hurt and despair. She was burdened by dark secrets just like me. I felt a sort of familiarity being with her, waiting here with her just so that she could have some company and not feel quite so alone.

As I looked around the waiting room, I couldn't help but notice the numerous posters plastered on the walls about birth control options. I'd never had to think about things like birth control, but as I sat there, my mind wandered to Knox, and I found myself thinking about birth control pills and condoms. I didn't know if or when anything might happen between us, or when Knox would be ready to take our physical relationship further, but I made a mental note to call and schedule an appointment with my gynecologist soon. Nerves danced in my belly at the thought of being intimate with him, but I knew I wanted him to be my first. Cold dread shivered down my spine. God, what would Belinda say? I shuddered at the thought. I was planning to have sex with one of our group members. Nothing about this situation was normal, but I didn't care because it felt right. And I was tired of being too careful, barely living these last few years. I wanted to be with Knox. Plain and simple. And I thought he wanted to be with me, too, as resistant as he'd been about taking our relationship further. We were making real progress and I wouldn't stop things now. And I'd need to make sure we were prepared so I didn't find myself in a situation like Amanda, with an unplanned pregnancy. Knox had enough mouths to feed. I wouldn't add a baby to mix.

I hadn't expected to go into the exam room with her, but when the nurse called her name, Amanda looked at me expectantly and waited for me to rise from my seat and join her. I could read the indecision in her eyes. She didn't want to be alone, and I couldn't blame her.

I held her hand while they performed an ultrasound and tears leaked from the corners of her eyes as she seen the tiny image of a baby inside her for the first time. The steady thump of the baby's heart was sure and strong.

The nurse estimated the baby to almost five months along, based on her measurements, which surprised Amanda. Her own calculations had been off. She was due in the spring.

'There's only one in there, right?' she asked the nurse, her voice high and almost panicked.

The nurse and I both smiled. 'Yes, there's just one baby. And he or she looks to be growing just fine. Did you want to know the sex?'

'Yes, please,' Amanda said.

'You're having a girl.'

I held her hand while she cried, her eyes fixed on the screen. It seemed Amanda wouldn't be alone any longer.

Helpful deed done for the day, I dropped Amanda off at home and texted Knox as I sat on the bus alone. Being around someone even more alone and lonely than myself all day had inspired a visit. I missed him.

Chapter Nine

McKenna

When I arrived at Knox's place, Tucker had already gone to bed, but Knox, Jaxon, and Luke all sat together in the living room. While they were normally so good-natured, tonight the mood felt tense. I toed off my shoes at the welcome mat and ventured in to see what they were discussing.

Luke sat on the sofa with his head hanging in his hands. Jaxon and Knox were perched in the arm chairs facing him, all of their expressions sour.

'Do you want to talk about it or are you going to keep moping around like someone kicked you in the balls?' Jaxon asked, looking squarely at Luke.

'Cool it, Jax,' Knox warned. 'Luke? You wanna talk?'

Luke peered up, his eyes wandering over to mine and then back to his brothers. I sat down next to him. 'Everything okay?' I asked.

He shrugged. 'Just girl problems,' he said, releasing a heavy sigh. 'Mollie broke up with me.'

I hadn't known that he had a girlfriend, but perhaps this was the reason he'd once asked me about how to make a girl's first time special. I still got a happy little feeling remembering how he'd opened up to me. 'I'm sorry.' I squeezed his hand.

'If Knox has taught us anything, it's that there are plenty of girls to go around. There's no sense getting your panties in a twist over this one. So pull your tampon out and man up,' Jaxon said, rising from the chair. 'And on that note, I'm going to bed. You guys are depressing.'

Knox frowned, watching Jaxon retreat up the stairs. 'Ignore him, Luke. Jax is an asshole.'

Luke's twisted expression relaxed slightly. 'How do you know when you're in love?' he asked Knox.

This should be interesting. I waited, breathless, to hear his answer.

Knox's brows drew together. 'You just do.' He hesitated for a few seconds, running his hand over the back of his neck, looking deep in thought, like he was trying to put into words whatever was churning inside his head. 'I guess you know when you want to spend time with the girl, protect her, and take care of her.'

My heart melted at hearing his description of love. We might not be there yet, but I hoped we were on our way.

'Like you are with McKenna?' Luke asked.

Knox's dark eyes met mine, and all the oxygen was ripped from my lungs. He didn't say anything else, he just watched me for several long moments while my heart pounded steadily. The warmth of hot adrenaline pushed through my veins. He was looking at me like he wanted to do unspeakable things to me and I was staring back at him, challenging him to take whatever he wanted. He already had my heart.

'Knox?' I asked, breaking the heavy silence. 'Will you give us a minute?' I tipped my head toward Luke. I wanted to talk to him alone and I might spontaneously combust if Knox kept looking at me like that, all dark and hungry.

'Sure.' Knox rose from the arm chair. 'I'll just go check on Tuck.'

Luke released a heavy sigh full of sorrow. I scooted closer to him on the couch. 'You okay, bud?'

'Yeah.' He flashed me a weak smile. 'This love shit sucks, though.'

'What happened with Mollie?'

He shrugged. 'She acted like she was into me, we went on a couple dates, and then I heard at school today she was seeing this other guy the entire time.'

'Then she wasn't worth your time. You're an amazing guy, Luke, thoughtful, smart, funny, and handsome. High school can be brutal, but you'll be at college soon and trust me, you'll be beating the girls off with a stick.' I grinned wickedly at him.

He laughed. 'Yeah, right. If I can even afford college. Every time I bring it up, Knox changes the subject. I've been applying to every scholarship I can find, but they're really competitive and so far, I haven't been offered a single one. I'm screwed without some financial help, no matter how good my grades are. My high school offers a scholarship to the valedictorian, which I have a good shot at – but it's a thousand bucks. What will that get me? Books for one semester?' He shook his head in defeat.

It crushed me to know that his future hung in the balance like that. 'I wish there was something I could do to help,' I pondered out loud.

'Just having you around helps. There's way too much testosterone in this house.'

I couldn't argue with that. 'Well, I plan on being around for a while. Someone's got to keep Knox in line.'

Descending down the stairs, Knox glanced our way. 'Did I hear my name?'

'Nope,' Luke and I said at the same time, sharing a secretive smile.

'Well, I guess I'm gonna go up, too, 'Luke said. 'Night, guys, and thanks, McKenna.'

'Night, Lukey!' I gave him a kiss on his cheek and watched him wander up the stairs before turning to face Knox. 'How was Tucker?'

'Sound asleep.' He sat down next to me. 'Is Luke alright?'

I nodded. 'Yeah. I just think there's a lot on his mind. Girls, how to pay for college….'

Knox blew out a frustrated breath. 'Fuck. Tell me about it. It's been keeping me up at night.'

I hadn't meant to add to his stress load, only to tell him how my conversation with Luke went. Knox hung his head in his hands and I moved closer so I could rub his shoulders. 'Don't worry. It'll all work out somehow.'

His head lifted until his intense gaze met mine. My fingers paused on his shoulders. 'That's just it. Nothing just works out around here unless I figure it out. And I've been trying for the last year to figure out how in the hell I'm going to help Luke pay for college and so far I've come up with jack shit nothing, so unless you have an extra fifty grand laying around, it won't just magically work out.' I could see the defeat written all over his features. He felt like a failure. He had three little lives depending on him and he wanted the best he could provide. 'I'm sorry.' His tone softened. 'I don't mean to take it out on you.' Considering that his usual way of taking out stress was by sleeping with random women, I would take sarcasm any day.

'It's okay. I know you're under a lot of pressure. I'm here to help however you need me.' I couldn't imagine being in his position. I only had to budget for myself and even that was tricky in an expensive city like Chicago.

'Thanks, Kenna.' He sat back against the sofa, pulling me closer. 'It's good to see you feeling better. What'd you do today?'

'I took Amanda to the doctor for a prenatal appointment. She's having a girl. They said the baby is healthy and progressing nicely.'

'That's good,' he said, grabbing the TV remote.

'Why didn't you tell me the truth about Amanda?'

He glanced up at me, remorse flashing in his eyes. 'I'm sorry. I should have. I just didn't want to give you something to worry about when I knew I had it under control.'

'She propositioned you?'

He nodded. 'There was no temptation there. None. I told you, I'm handling it. And I've got someone better I'm waiting for.' He laced our fingers together, his palm resting against mine, warm and solid.

'Should we go upstairs?' I whispered, suddenly feeling bold and wanting some privacy with him.

'I thought we'd hang out down here, maybe watch a movie or something.'

'Oh, okay.' I tried to hide the disappointment in my voice, but failed.

Knox flipped through the selection of available movies for rent and let me pick a romantic comedy I'd been waiting to see for several months. I curled against his side and he held me while we watched the sugary-sweet interactions playing out on the screen. They seemed so far from real life. At least far-removed from my life and Knox's. In my experiences, real life and love were incredibly messy affairs. That was what I knew. Maybe that was why I was so comfortable with Knox. He'd been through hell and back, too, and we recognized those deep scars in each other.

Throughout the entire movie Knox kept things purely platonic. His arms were wrapped around me, strong and sure, but the few times I'd tried to let my hands wander to touch him, his stomach, his thigh...he would tighten his grip around me, holding me in place and effectively preventing me from touching him. It was incredibly frustrating and only left me worked up and buzzing unfulfilled energy inside me.

For two hours I lay there in his arms, his chest rising and falling steadily against my back, his breath warming the back of my neck. Various scenarios played out in my head. I imagined rolling towards him, unbuckling his belt and touching him again. What would he do then? The realization that he may stop me, that he might reject me, prevented me from making my move.

Once the credits rolled, I climbed from my warm spot next to him on the couch and stood, stretching. 'Should we go up to bed?'

Knox stood up, watching me warily. 'You're sleeping over?'

'Is that okay?' *God, why was he acting so weird tonight?*

He hesitated, looking down at the floor.

'Why are you acting like you don't want me here?'

He didn't respond, he just continued staring down at the floor between our feet.

'Knox?'

'This is hard for me, being near you and knowing I can't have you,' he admitted softly.

I wanted to tell him he could have me, anytime, anyplace. I'd gotten brief glimpses of how good we could be together and I wanted more. 'You have me,' I whispered.

He crossed the room and pulled me into his arms. 'I know. I'm sorry, angel. I have a lot on my mind and I don't want to fuck this up with you. That's all.'

'Do you want me to go?' I looked up at him, blinking.

'No. Stay. Please?'

I nodded and let him guide me up the stairs.

Once I'd brushed my teeth and changed into a T-shirt of Knox's, I stood beside the bed, watching while he pulled his shirt off over his head and stripped out of his jeans. His body was a work of art, complete with sculpted lines and rugged muscles that I wanted to touch and lick. He evoked strange feelings inside me that no man had before. It was an almost animal attraction that brought out a new and viscerally sexual side of me.

'Knox?'

'Hmm?' He asked, folding his jeans and tossing them on top of his dresser.

I found my courage and took a step closer, tugging on the hem of my borrowed T-shirt. 'When we said we were gonna do this, a real relationship…to me that meant everything that came along with a relationship.' Several long moments ticked by while my heart beat thudded dully in my chest.

'Say we do this thing for real – then what?' Frustrated, his hands tore through his hair, leaving it in a sexy disarray.

'What do you mean? We agree to be there for each other, we both try.'

'And if I fuck up? If I hurt you….' He stared blankly at the wall above my head. 'I couldn't…I wouldn't chance that.' I knew there was more he wasn't saying. I'd already been through too much with my parents. I was damaged and he wouldn't be part of contributing to my hurt any more than he already had. I hated that I could never seem to escape my past, no matter how hard I worked.

'Isn't that for me to decide?'

His eyes slid back to mine. 'You believe in me way too much.'

'Someone's got to, Knox. I've seen the real you. The one you keep hidden from everyone else. You're a good man, despite what you want me to believe.'

'You refuse to see the bad in me.'

'So tell me, then. What's so bad about you?' I was edging into dangerous territory. We'd never really covered his background in detail and I wasn't sure I could handle it, but I was putting on my bravest front to show him that I wouldn't be scared off. Who cared if prickles of sweat were forming against the back of my neck and my knees felt shaky? It was a conversation that needed to happen.

'You really want to hear the shit I've done?'

Suddenly losing my nerve, my lips parted, but no sound came out.

Knox took a step closer, his gaze hardening. 'You want to hear that I fucked a mother and her eighteen-year-old daughter in the same day? That I broke up my buddy's engagement when I accepted a blowjob from his fiancée? That because of this sick need inside me I've pushed every boundary, every limit? That I enjoy anal sex and the occasional ménage? Is that what you want to hear? You can't handle me, angel. I can barely fucking handle me.'

The air whooshed from my lungs, my confidence vanishing. For the first time I began to doubt him – us – my belief that this could work falling away like a veil in the wind. He would want things I couldn't possibility give him.

'Say something,' he ordered, taking a predatory step closer.

'I get it, okay? You made your point. You're experienced. I'm not.'

'That wasn't my point. Not at all.' He hung his head, looking down at the floor, his hands returning to his hair once again. 'I'm sick, not a man worthy of you,' he whispered.

My heart broke for him. He deserved love and acceptance even if he couldn't see that. 'The things you've done don't scare me. I just worry I won't measure up to your past.'

He stepped closer, wrapping a hand around my hip to draw me nearer until we were just inches apart. It didn't escape my notice that he was dressed in only a pair of black boxer briefs. 'You have it backwards. My past doesn't measure up to you.' His voice was whispery soft and his mouth was brushing against my ear, sending delicious little shivers racing down my spine. He pressed a tender kiss against the side of my neck and my head fell back, my body craving more. His warm tongue slid against my pulse point, which was fluttering wildly. 'I can read your fear, your uncertainty. You're not ready for this.'

Finding my voice, I whispered, 'So show me.'

'You don't know what you're saying, what you're agreeing to.'

We'd spoken only briefly about his dominant nature, but that word hung in the air all around us, its hidden meaning permeating my every pore. Maybe I couldn't handle his brand of physical affection. But what he'd shown me so far had been tender and intimate. Would sex with Knox really be so different? His tastes and desires were unknown to me, but most of me found that exciting. Nerves raced through my belly as he nipped at my neck. 'If we do this, Knox…have a real relationship, you'd have to show me….' I breathed, finding my courage.

He squeezed me tighter. 'If we do this, you have to tell Brian about us.'

I giggled. Such an alpha male thing to say, laying his claim to me and wanting it known by all. 'Of course I will. But stop avoiding this conversation. '

'What conversation are we having, McKenna?' He sucked the skin at the base of my neck, pressing sweet kisses against my collarbone.

'Sex,' I murmured.

'You're not ready yet,' he said. I pulled back and gave him a quizzical look. Was he serious right now? 'I'll know when you're ready,' he continued. 'You need to trust me.' His hands cupped my cheeks and he pressed a kiss to my forehead. I didn't want to be treated like a china doll. I'd waited long enough for this moment in my life and I was sure.

'And you need to trust me.' I might be damaged, but I was stronger than he was giving me credit for. I could handle this. Couldn't I?

He watched me with hooded eyes, taking stock of everything he saw – every emotion and stray thought racing through my brain. My entire body was alive and humming. It was as though he could see straight into me and read all my inner thoughts. It was the oddest sensation.

'Tell me what you want to know,' he said, brushing the hair back from my face.

My stomach was coiled tight and nervous energy shot through my veins. Something was about to happen. I'd pushed him and now I needed to be sure I really was ready. 'You seem so sure. And I don't know what I'm doing. I just need to know that's okay with you.'

'That's a turn on, trust me. I can be a little dominating in the bedroom.'

Finally, we were discussing the elephant in the room. 'A dominant? Like…you want a submissive?' My entire body was tingling. I had to know what I was signing up for.

'Mmm, not exactly.' His large palm curled around the back of my neck, his thumb stroking the skin there. 'I just like taking charge. Nothing extreme, I promise.'

My belly tightened. 'I'm not into pain, Knox.'

'That's not my thing at all, angel. You'd never have to worry about me hurting you.' His voice was sincere, and his warm honey eyes were loving and kind, but that didn't stop the uncertainty raging inside me.

'What do you want, then?'

'Control. To show you pleasure.'

His words sent a jab of lust straight between my thighs and I let out a whimper. Something about this man, his desire to bring me pleasure, lit me up from the inside out. If he had a trace of dominance, perhaps I had a trace of submissiveness.

'You like that, don't you, angel?' he asked. I nodded slowly, biting my lip as I gazed up at him. 'Soon,' he promised. 'My self-control is almost non-existent where you're concerned.'

'Everyone's had you. But I can't? How's that fair?'

'I'm giving you everything.'

'By not giving me any?' I argued.

'Stop, McKenna. You don't know what you're saying.'

'I do, though, that's the thing. I want this with you. And not this pseudo friend-zone you've placed me in. I want everything. I want to be loved, cherished, and made to feel like a woman, your woman, not your little sister.'

'If you were my sister, I'd be put in jail for the things I want to do to you.'

My heart stuttered. He did want the same things as me, I could see it in his eyes. 'If I'm pushing you – if this is about your addiction, or because I'm your counselor….'

'It's not.' He stepped closer.

'Then what is it?'

'Brian told me.'

'He told you….' I paused. He needed to fill in the blank because I failed to see what Brian had to do with any of this.

Chapter Ten

Knox

McKenna was looking at me expectantly, waiting for me to explain. *Shit*. 'When I came to see you when you were sick, Brian pulled me aside. He wanted to know what my intentions were with you.'

A tiny crease formed across her forehead. 'And...what are they?'

'I told him you were sick and I was simply there to take care of you. He thinks I'm a sexual sociopath. He was looking at me like I was going to shove my dick down your throat while you're sick, and I assured him I could keep it in my pants.'

She chewed on her lip and waited. 'What did he say?' she asked.

'He told me.' She waited, breathless, her eyes locked on mine. 'McKenna, are you a virgin?'

She sucked in a shuddery breath and her gaze fell from mine. I didn't want her to feel ashamed or embarrassed, and shit, I probably shouldn't have just sprung this on her, but we needed to discuss this. It didn't help that we were having this conversation dressed as we were – me in my underwear and her in just a T-shirt. But she needed to see that she wasn't ready for me.

'Does it matter?' she asked, clenching her fists at her sides.

'It does to me.'

'So this *is* about my inexperience. I'm sorry to disappoint you.'

She thought she was disappointing me, which made zero sense. 'You don't know what you're talking about. I'm not disappointed. I'm fucking terrified. The thought of being the first to touch you, the first man to be inside you, to penetrate your tight pussy, makes me insane, but I'm scared I can't be what you need.'

'What do you mean?' Sapphire blue eyes, wide with curiosity, blinked up at mine. 'What do you think I need?'

'You need someone to be gentle and careful with you, someone who's soft and slow.'

'You could try….' she murmured.

'I don't trust myself.'

'I trust you.' Those same eyes, now blazing with determination, stared into mine. 'I'm here because I trust you.'

She looked so beautiful, so soft and sweet, standing there in my faded gray T-shirt, feet bare and toes painted pink. And hearing her confess that she trusted me with something so sacred tugged at something deep inside me. Confessing some of my background has been a scare tactic. But the look in her eyes didn't match the expression of a scared little girl. She needed to understand how fucked up I was. I couldn't let myself tarnish her perfection. And I would. I would take every last bit of her innocence and obliterate it just to quench my own desire.

Exercising my last ounce of self-control, I closed the distance between us and pressed a kiss to her mouth. 'I'm not budging on this. I don't think you're ready yet.' It was either walk away now or throw her down on my bed and have my way with her.

Her hands flew to her hips. 'You also didn't think you had a problem with sex, and you fought me on getting STD testing done, and I know pushing you on both was the right thing. I get that you're scared, but Knox….'

I looked down, popping the knuckles in my fingers. 'There's something else,' I admitted. She looked at me quizzically. 'I knew when you didn't say anything last time that you were probably inexperienced, because usually it's the first thing girls comment on....'

Shit. She still wasn't catching on. I was going to have to spell it out for her. 'I'm, um, a lot bigger than average.' I sounded like a cocky asshole, but I wasn't bragging. I wasn't trying to impress her. I was trying to warn her. To ensure she understood that this probably wouldn't be fun for her.

A slow smile uncurled on McKenna's lips. Not the reaction I'd been expecting. It made me wonder if perhaps she had noticed my size, either that or she was remembering it fondly now. But I wasn't trying to be cute. I'd had one girl actually tell me she needed to take a muscle relaxer before she'd let me fuck her. She was a little dramatic, but I wasn't kidding that nearly every woman I'd been with had commented on my size – I was a lot to handle, and they weren't virgins.

I hadn't been with a virgin since high school and I didn't exactly remember the experience favorably. I didn't take pleasure in causing pain. It wasn't something I wanted to repeat, but now with McKenna standing before me looking vulnerable and needy, I wouldn't reject her and I certainly wouldn't push her into the arms of another man. As much as I might have been fighting it, I knew it had to be me. If not tonight, then soon. Neither of us were good at waiting, it seemed.

McKenna pouted, her lower lip jutting out.

'Come here,' I ordered.

She hesitantly stepped forward, her fingers still playing with the hem of the shirt.

'What do you have to do tomorrow?'

'I'm working at the teen shelter, but not until ten in the morning. Why?'

I smoothed my hands up and down her arms. 'You'll probably be sore. I wanted to make sure you don't have anything too strenuous planned.'

Her pulse thundered in her neck as if she realized for the first time that we really were going to do this. My dick had gotten the memo, too, lengthening in my boxers and growing heavy against my thigh. He would have to wait his fucking turn. I would do everything in my power to make sure McKenna was as wet and ready as possible before I took the precious gift she was offering. It was the least I could do. She was giving me something that could never be replaced. There were no do-overs.

I was never nervous before sex, but my own heart was thudding like a damn drum in my chest. The significance of this moment hit me hard. But I was like a hungry lion and she'd pushed me too far and now I needed a taste.

'I need to know your limits,' I said, watching her fidget.

'My limits?' That tiny crease between her brow was back.

'I need to know if there's something you're uncomfortable with.'

She chewed on her lip. There was something on her mind, but she was afraid to voice it.

'Tell me,' I commanded, my voice steady.

She wet her lips, stalling for more time. 'I don't like, um, oral sex.'

'To give it or receive it?' I questioned, raising one dark brow. This was interesting, and not what I'd expected her to say.

'Receiving it,' she managed to blurt out, looking down at the floor under my watchful stare.

'Why not?'

Her little hands balled into fists at her sides like she was afraid to admit whatever it was on her mind.

'Has anyone ever done that to you before, angel?'

She shook her head.

I sucked in a hiss of a breath and cursed. Shit, that only made me want to do it more. 'Why do you think you wouldn't like it?'

'Be-because I can't imagine I'll taste good and…I would hate for you to think I smell or taste bad.'

She was self-conscious, but she had no reason to be. I was certain she'd taste delicious, salty and sweet just like a woman should. I would enjoy showing her just how very wrong she was. I inhaled against the side of her neck. 'I love your scent,' I promised. 'And I'm certain you'll taste delicious. Real males like that taste, McKenna.' She sucked in a breath. 'Let me worship your pussy,' I breathed against her throat, causing her to break out in chill bumps. She shook her head. 'That's unacceptable.' She might have said this was something she didn't want, but it was the first thing I wanted to start with, limits be damned.

She opened her mouth to protest, then closed it with a squeak.

That's what I thought. 'Anything else?'

'When you said you liked, um….' She heaved in a breath and held it, too uncomfortable to continue. I could only assume she was talking about my rant on enjoying anal sex.

'I won't be doing that with you. At least not yet.' I wasn't sure McKenna was the kind of girl to ever be ready for that kind of total domination, letting me take her most private of places, but I wouldn't decide for her, not now. She constantly surprised me and perhaps between the sheets wouldn't be any different.

She nodded, relief washing over her features.

Leaning down to brush my mouth against her neck, I whispered, 'If this is what you need, I'll take care of you. I wanted to show you I could wait, that this was more to me than sex.'

She pulled back slightly to meet my eyes. 'I already know this is more for you. You don't do relationships, or bring girls home to meet your brothers, and I'm guessing you don't often volunteer or go out of your way for a girl. You've already shown me with your actions what I mean to you. It's time for both of us to be brave.'

I nodded. It was time to be brave. Grasping her hips, I walked her backwards to the bed and when the backs of her knees touched the edge of the mattress, she sat.

Wide blue eyes stared up at me as she waited, wondering what came next. Her gaze wandered lower, looking at the bulge in my boxer briefs.

'Do you want to touch me?' I asked.

She swallowed and nodded, her head bobbing up and down.

The urge to watch her pretty mouth around my cock pulsed inside me, causing an almost unbearable pressure. Now that I knew McKenna's intentions and desires, there would be no stopping now. We may not have sex tonight, but we were both ready for more. I nodded once, indicating that she could do what she wanted. McKenna hesitated, her hands twisting in her lap. I decided to play nice and help her out, tugging my boxer briefs down slowly. Her eyes locked onto my movements. My cock sprang free and she sucked in a shuddery breath. Using my right hand, I grasped my dick and stroked it slowly, showing her what I wanted her to do.

McKenna's hands uncurled in her lap and she gingerly brought them to my stomach, lightly tracing my abdominal muscles. I remembered back to the first time she'd touched me. She'd been so curious, yet so uncertain. It was an incredibly hot combination. With my heart pounding in my chest, I fought for patience, for self-control, when I was so used to exercising neither.

Soon, McKenna's hands wandered lower as her bravery blossomed. Biting her bottom lip firmly between her teeth, she finally closed her fist around me and a low growl escaped the back of my throat. Using both hands to stroke me up and down, McKenna did so slowly, as if savoring the feel of my cock in her hands. Her fingertips didn't close around me and I watched in wonder as she worked me over, using her palms, her fingertips, to pleasure me. It was the slowest, most erotic handjob I'd ever received. My knees trembled and my stomach muscles were clenched tight.

Her hands continued rubbing my cock, one hand even venturing under to lightly cup my balls. I could let her do this all day, but something inside me wanted to push her just a little bit more. And I knew McKenna wanted that, too. She wanted the full experience, to see my dominant side that I'd kept hidden from her.

'Get it wet,' I said.

Her eyes snapped up to meet mine, confusion evident between her brows. She glanced to the bedside table, then the dresser, looking for some type of lubricant. 'I – I don't have anything,' she murmured.

'Yes, you do.'

Realization flashed across her features.

I wanted to see her wet her palm with her mouth, or even hotter, the moisture that was certain to be between her legs, but instead she did something totally unexpected.

She brought her full lips to the head of my cock, and pressed a soft kiss there. I let out a ragged groan, fighting the desire to work myself deep into her throat. As much as I wanted to take control, I needed to let her do this at her own pace.

Satisfied with my reaction, McKenna did it again, this time letting the warmth of her tongue lave over my rock hard flesh, eliciting another moan from me. As she grew even bolder, she let her tongue wander the length of my shaft, doing just what I'd asked, getting me nice and wet. Her hands slid easily up and over me, pushing my pleasure to new levels.

Leaning forward, McKenna took me into the warmth of her mouth, her full lips suckling against my sensitive skin.

Fuck.

She might be inexperienced, but she certainly knew how to bring me to my knees. Maybe it was because of her lack of experience that I valued this so much. It meant even more. She was going out on a limb, pushing all her boundaries – for me. It did heady things to my ego. But tonight wasn't about me, it was about her. Lifting her chin with one hand, I fell free of her mouth, my dick glistening with her salvia and her lips damp and swollen.

'You're too damn good at that,' I murmured, stroking her cheek.

She beamed up at me, clearly satisfied with my compliment. I wanted to make her feel comfortable and ready for all the new experiences I had in store for her.

'Lay back.'

McKenna obeyed, scooting further up the bed, her T-shirt bunching up around her waist as she moved, the sight of her plain white cotton panties taunting me. She watched me with wide eyes as I slowly peeled her panties down her legs, exposing her most sensitive area, and dropped them on the floor at my feet.

I kissed her inner thigh and felt her shudder. Working my way up her body with gentle nips and kisses, I took my time, listening to her body's silent signals. The dip of her belly when my mouth tickled her hip bone, her undulating hips when I got close to her center. A few minutes more and I knew she'd be practically begging me to touch her there. But not yet. I removed the T-shirt over her head and continued tasting her skin. First mouthing the heavy weight of her breast, then a chaste kiss in the center of her breast bone. McKenna's frustrated whimper told me I wasn't focusing on the areas she needed me. Good thing I was about to give her everything she could handle. And then some.

I kissed my way to the tip of her breast and bit down, carefully using my teeth to tug the bud of her nipple. A surprised gasp pushed past McKenna's lips and I couldn't help the satisfied growl that escaped mine. Twisted need and desire spiked through me. She was finally beginning to understand that I was in control, that she'd given me her body and pushed me into this. I needed to do this my way.

I began licking her nipples in the same rhythmic pattern I wanted to lick her clit, eliciting soft groans and pants from her.

Every little moment with her, watching her discover the pleasure I could give her, was like a small victory. She was giving herself to me. Happiness surged through me. She squirmed, struggling against the mattress, her writhing hips making it difficult for me to give her breasts the focus they deserved. Even if her head didn't want my mouth moving south, her entire body disagreed.

Lifting my head from one breast, my eyes met hers. 'Are you sure you don't want me to lick your pussy?' McKenna squeaked out something unintelligible and I chuckled against her neck. 'Let me take care of you.' I trailed my mouth lower, kissing her navel as I moved down her body. 'Just a taste,' I whispered against her pubic bone.

Her scent was maddening – purely feminine and entirely too tempting. I wasn't going to be able to go slow. My mouth closed around her folds and I sucked – hard – against her clit. McKenna's hips shot off the bed and her hands tugged at my hair. But I didn't let up. I rubbed my tongue against her until her muscles were trembling and her moans were almost loud enough to wake my brothers. I lifted my head just long enough to give her a pillow. 'Here. Scream into this if you need to.'

Her cheeks flushed crimson. 'Oh my God. Was I being loud?'

My grin was the only answer she got before I dropped my lips to her sweet flesh again and gave her a gentle kiss. I considered teasing her – pointing out that just fifteen minutes ago this had been on her list of hard limits. And now I was pretty sure it was her new favorite thing. But I kept that piece of knowledge to myself, pride swelling in my chest.

After a few more teasing flicks of my tongue I bit down on her clit, forcing a cry from her lips and the first orgasm to crash through her, her body lightly trembling as she laced her fingers in my hair, pulling me closer. I continued licking and softly kissing her as the aftershocks pulsed through her. It was agony knowing how good it would feel to be inside her when she came, her tight little body throbbing around me.

'Knox...,' she groaned, out of breath, 'That was....'

'Shh.' I pressed the tip of one finger against her opening, finding her wet and ready. I wasn't done with her. Not by a long shot. I eased my middle finger forward and watched for her reaction. Her eyelids, suddenly heavy, began to fall closed. Inside, her body was hot and silky and never in my life had I appreciated a woman trusting me with her so completely.

Pushing slowly in and out, allowing her to get used to the sensations, I carefully added a second finger. I felt her tense and a brief pinched expression flashed across her features. 'Is this okay?' I murmured, kissing her inner thigh.

She nodded tightly.

She might have thought she was ready, but the way she was clamping down on my fingers assured me she needed more time. Knowing I couldn't take what she was offering tonight, my goal became to see how many times I could make her come.

Using the pad of my thumb, I circled her clit while my fingers continued pumping in and out of her. She clawed at the sheets, pushing her mouth against the pillow, and let out a long shuddering moan as another orgasm wracked her body from the inside out.

Chapter Eleven

McKenna

Blinking open heavy eyelids, I struggled to make sense of my surroundings. I didn't remember where I was, what day it was, or even my own name. I felt like I had been drugged. I stretched and turned my head and saw Knox's sleeping form lying next to me. Memories of last night came rushing back with vivid clarity. Knox's hot mouth on my most sensitive parts, his fingers pumping into me…I shuddered at the memory.

I'd opened up and told Knox my feelings on taking our physical relationship to the next level, and while we hadn't had sex, it felt like we'd grown closer. I was happy, if not a little dazed by the whole experience.

A quick check of the clock told me it was still early, just after sunrise, and I rolled closer to Knox, snuggling in beside him.

Draping a heavy arm over me, he pulled me tightly against him. 'You okay, angel?' His sleep-laced voice was deep and husky.

'I'm fine,' I whispered, breathing in the masculine scent of his chest.

'I'm sorry about last night.'

I rolled onto my side and looked up at him. 'Sorry about what?' From my perspective, I should be the one apologizing. He'd pleasured me until I all but passed out from exhaustion and I hadn't taken care of him at all. A fact I felt a little guilty about.

'Are you sore?' he asked, his eyes like warm molten honey on mine.

I shook my head. At least I didn't think so.

'I was too rough with you,' he murmured, pressing a kiss to my forehead.

Memories of him biting me – my nipples and my clit – rushed back in full force. The press of his fingers roughly pushing into me. Knox thought I'd be upset, but I was relieved to see he hadn't treated me like a china doll. He'd lost himself in me, which was exactly what I wanted, considering I felt so out of control around him, too. Pressing my palm against his cheek, I returned his kiss. 'You bit me,' I said, fighting a smile.

'I know.'

'You said you weren't into pain.'

'Did it hurt?' The warmth and sincerity in his eyes nearly stole my voice. He was so beautiful, this confusing, troubled man.

'Well, no. Not really.'

'I just wanted you to understand that you were mine.'

'Oh.' My heart galloped. I was his. Body and soul. And falling deeper every day.

'Was last night okay, then?'

I nodded, my head bobbing up and down while he studied me. 'I liked it.' Liking it was an understatement, but the furrow creasing his brow told me not to press the issue.

'Are you sure you're alright with this?'

I knew he was asking more than his words conveyed. He was asking if I was okay with his nature – his dominant, take charge attitude in the bedroom. The truth was, I was more than okay with it. With Knox I felt like a woman. I liked him making the decisions and pushing me in ways I never dreamed. He was opening me up to new experiences, just like I was doing for him. 'Last night was perfect. I'm just sorry I fell asleep on you.'

He smiled, the playful gleam I loved returning to his eyes. 'Passed out was more like it.'

I gave him a shove, but his body was a solid wall of immovable muscle. What he'd said was true, though, I'd all but collapsed from exhaustion after the three powerful climaxes he'd given me. If this was what a sexual relationship with him was going to be like, I would be one happy girl.

'I gotta get the guys up and ready for school.' Knox kissed my lips and then climbed from the bed, treating me to a view of his firm backside as he moved across the room and began to dress.

I lazily stretched and then joined him, forcing my languid and relaxed body into yesterday's clothes before venturing downstairs.

I found the boys were already up and moving about.

'Dude, don't sit so close to the TV, Tuck,' Jaxon said, nudging Tucker's shoulder. 'You're gonna get a tan from that thing.'

I chuckled as I watched them. The glow of the television was casting a bluish hue over Tucker's little face, but he obeyed, scooting backwards on his butt. Knox might have been worried about the second oldest Bauer boy, but I could see that in his heart, Jax was one of the good guys. Or maybe I just had entirely too much faith. I'd always believed the same thing about Knox, too. Yet I couldn't help the inexplicable feeling that everything good was about to come crashing down around me in a messy heap.

'What are these?' I asked, sniffing a huge arrangement of pink carnations on my dining room table.

Brian appeared in the doorway after changing out of his suit and tie and into jeans. He'd arrived home from work just a few minutes after me.

I picked through the pink blossoms, hunting for a card. There wasn't one and somehow I couldn't really imagine Knox sending me pink carnations. Maybe blood red roses, but not these. And when would he have had the time? I'd just left his house this morning and I knew he'd worked all day, too.

Brian watched me curiously. 'They're from me.'

'Oh. What's the occasion?' I couldn't recall Brian ever giving me flowers...except the bouquet he'd had sent to the funeral home at my parents' wake. But those had been white daylilies. For a totally different reason.

'No occasion. I just wanted to....' He stopped himself and exhaled heavily. 'Come sit down with me.'

'Okay.' He was acting strange. I wondered if he'd caught the flu that was going around.

We sat side by side on the sofa, the TV playing softly in the background.

'I just wanted to apologize for everything lately. My behavior toward you, and fighting with Knox.' He lifted my hand from my lap and held it. 'I know you've been through a lot and I just want you to know I'll always be here for you. I'll be whatever you need, okay?'

'Okay. That's sweet of you, Bri.'

Neither of us could deny that something had changed between us since Knox had come into the picture. I remembered Knox's request that I tell Brian about us, but somehow I knew the moment wasn't right. He was trying to apologize, to make amends. He'd gotten me flowers, which was sweet, but not necessary. Giving a girl carnations wasn't a romantic gesture, was it? Pushing all that from my mind, I thanked him for the flowers and headed into the kitchen. 'Are you hungry?'

'Starved,' he confirmed.

We were like two ravenous lions come dinner time. We'd been that way since we were kids. Searching through the cabinets, we settled on grilled cheese sandwiches. We worked together in the kitchen, him grilling the sandwiches and me slicing some tomatoes that were about to go bad. It'd been a while since we'd enjoyed each other's company like this and I was happy to see the previous tension between us was all but gone.

Over gooey, cheesy sandwiches, Brian shoved an envelope at me. 'This came for you today.'

The return address was a law firm in Indiana.

My stomach dropped.

I didn't want to open it, knowing it was somehow related to my parents' accident. But the letter taunted me, capturing all of my attention.

Brian's sheepish look apologized for something over which he had no control. I wondered if this was the real reason for the flowers. He knew this would upset me – take me right back to that dark place I was in four years ago. Running to Chicago hadn't been enough. My past would follow me anywhere.

'Are you going to open it?' he asked, pulling my thoughts back to the present. I looked down at my plate. I'd picked apart my sandwich into little bits. So much for my appetite. 'What do you think it is?'

'Not sure,' I said, finding my voice. 'Probably something to do with their will.'

He nodded and pushed away his own plate. It must be sympathy pains or something since I knew we were both hungry when we'd sat down.

I'd yet to settle all my parents' legal affairs, since dealing with it bought up too many painful memories. I'd done the bare minimum, the funeral was planned, and with the help of Brian's mom and a local realtor, I'd sold the house I grew up in. The movers had packed everything and it was all still sitting in a storage unit in my hometown. All the rest, pension plan, retirement accounts, and insurance policies remained on the back burner, untouched. Dealing with it all would be too final, and I just wasn't ready to go there. I especially didn't like this envelope with its shiny gold embossment on my dining table looking up at me, reminding me. It felt like two sides of my life were intersecting. It was childish, but maybe if I just refused to open the envelope, I could pretend that none of this was happening.

For all my running, all my volunteer work to make things better in this world, I still had to face that there was a bitter force driving me. It scared me to realize that maybe running into Knox's arms had nothing to do with love. It was about me throwing myself into something even messier and uglier than my own past. It was simply another place to hide.

'You're not going to open it, are you?' Brian asked, pulling me from my somber thoughts.

He knew me all too well. 'Wasn't planning on it, no.' I pushed the offending paper away, knowing it was pointless. I'd likely find it on my dresser later.

'Can I ask you something?' He glanced down at his plate, picking at the remnants of his sandwich.

'Sure.'

'Have you and Knox….' His forehead creased. 'Are you still….'

'Brian, that's none of your business.'

'You are,' he said, his voice certain.

I wanted to yell at him for interfering and telling Knox I was a virgin in the first place, but faced with the awkwardness of the conversation, I chickened out. Closing my eyes, I drew a deep breath.

'Wow. I'm surprised. Even after all those nights you've spent there?'

I released my breath in a huff. 'I know you have a hard time believing this, but Knox really is a good guy. He would never do something I wasn't ready for. And he's been in recovery, so sex really wasn't on the table for either of us.'

'But it is now?' His eyebrow quirked up. 'And you're right, I do have a hard time believing that.'

A heavy silence fell over us and I considered ripping open the envelope just for something to distract me from this awful moment.

Brian leaned closer, planting his elbows on the table. 'So if you haven't fully given yourself to him, does that mean….' He hesitated, drawing a deep breath. 'Do you think there'd ever be a chance for us?'

I wanted to set him straight, tell him once and for all it was never going to happen between us, but sitting there, looking into his bright blue eyes, something in me couldn't crush him. He'd done too much for me. Still, I didn't want to leave him with false hope. That wasn't fair to him. 'Brian, I'm dating Knox. You should date other people, too.' It was my subtle way of telling him he needed to stop pining for me.

'Your dad, your parents, they would have wanted you with me. You know that, right?' he asked. I swallowed a bitter lump in my throat. 'They joked we'd get married someday from the time we were six years old, McKenna.'

Fighting back tears, I excused myself to my bedroom while Brian called out my name. Bringing my parents into this wasn't fair. He knew my life's mission was to try and honor them in all things. My chosen career field, how I spent my time, but I'd never factored in who I dated. Realizing Brian was right sucked. My parents had adored him.

I fell back heavily onto my mattress with a thud. Today had been too much. I couldn't deal with the mystery envelope regarding my parents and Brian's declaration that I was dishonoring them by choosing the wrong man.

Part of me knew I couldn't hide in my bed forever, but most of me wanted to try.

Chapter Twelve

McKenna

The next several days passed in a blur. Between working, volunteering, and helping Amanda get around – everything from taking her to doctor's appointments to shopping for maternity clothes to buying prenatal vitamins, I'd barely had time to see Knox. And our alone time together had all but disappeared.

But tonight that was going to change, because Jaxon and Luke were taking Tucker out to dinner and then to their high school's basketball game, meaning Knox and I would have the house to ourselves for a couple of hours. It was exactly what I'd needed after a trying week.

I found Knox alone upstairs in his bedroom, sitting on the edge of his bed with his sketchbook open in his lap, looking deep in thought.

'Hi,' I greeted him.

'Hey.' He closed the book and crossed the room, drawing me into his arms. 'Everything okay? You look exhausted.'

Leave it to Knox to immediately pick up on how drained and crummy I felt. 'I'm fine. It was just a long week.'

'Yeah? And how many hours did you work this week?'

I quickly did the math in my head. 'Mmm, somewhere around seventy, I'd guess.'

'McKenna,' he groaned, holding my shoulders and positioning me so he could meet my eyes. The dark circles lining them wouldn't help my case. But Knox couldn't understand how one simple letter from a lawyer back home could send me into a tailspin. It had been easier to work and volunteer than to sit at home with the constant reminder staring me in the face.

Knox pulled me over to the small sofa on the far end of his bedroom and we sat down. He looked at me intently. 'What?' I asked finally.

'Just like you help me, I want to help you.'

'What do you mean?'

'You've got to stop running.'

'What makes you think that's what I'm doing?'

'You work seventy hours a week volunteering, you don't do anything for yourself. When's the last time you did something normal girls your age enjoy? Like go shopping or get your nails done?'

I stiffened at his implication that I wasn't a normal girl. 'How's that fair? When's the last time you did something a normal twenty-two year old guy would do?'

He smirked. 'Not the same thing, angel. I have custody of three boys. Don't bring my shit into this. We're talking about you.'

'I happen to like volunteering, and I like being here with you guys. I have no desire to go out and party it up like a twenty-one year old.'

'But someday you might. And you might regret not doing all the things young people are supposed to do.'

Was he speaking from experience? He'd certainly missed out on enough being responsible for his brothers. Though his sexploits more than made up for that deficit. 'I'm not going to regret anything.' I already lived with enough regret over my choices that fateful day I'd lost my parents. There wasn't room for more in my world. 'Serving others is the only thing that keeps me sane. The only thing that makes me feel okay with being me,' I whispered.

'I get that.'

'Then don't ask me to change.'

'I want you to find balance – that's all.' Knox wrapped one hand around my knee and gave it a gentle squeeze. His touch was all that was needed to reassure me. He wasn't trying to force me to change or make me feel guilty about my choices.

'I want that, too,' I admitted.

'One step at a time. Right, angel?'

I grinned up at him wryly. It was the same thing I'd said to him once about his addiction. 'Right.' I was suddenly feeling like the patient rather than the counselor. This was new.

'There's something that scares me, McKenna.' Knox ran a hand through his wayward hair, meeting my eyes with a worried stare. 'One day you're going to forgive yourself and let go of all this hurt you carry around. You're going to wake up and realize I'm all wrong for you.'

Knox was the only one to call me out on my obsessive tendencies. I avoided my life. I avoided dealing with my emotions and grief. Not even Brian was brave enough to tell me the truth. I appreciated his honesty, but he was wrong. I'd always want him. He made me feel alive and secure. Like maybe I could finally stop running from my past.

'And when all that happens, you're going to want someone nice and normal,' he continued.

'Let me guess, someone like Brian?'

'The thought has crossed my mind, yes. He's in love with you, McKenna.'

The crushing weight of the knowledge that he was right hit me square in the chest. Knox was looking at me like he could see straight through me. I could not have felt more exposed if I'd been sitting there completely naked. How did he not only understand me so well, but also get my complicated relationship with Brian? Feeling vulnerable and needy, I curled into his side, needing his warmth, his protection from the muddled mess my life had become. Knox pulled me closer, lifting my mouth to his while my pulsed thrummed violently in the base of my throat.

I didn't try and explain away my feelings, I didn't even tell him that I wasn't going anywhere, but I did decide then and there it was time to show him how deeply my feelings for him ran.

Chapter Thirteen

Knox

Unable to resist the swell of her full mouth quivering so close to mine, I lowered my lips to hers.

A kiss that was meant to be innocent quickly turned heated. McKenna whimpered and opened her mouth to mine, our tongues tangling wildly as her hands pushed into my hair. She nipped my lower lip, tugging it with her teeth to pull me closer.

She was a woman in need and I was just a man. A man who hadn't been laid in God knows how long. I needed to feel her heat surround me. Gripping her ass, I lifted her from the sofa and moved her to my lap. She wrapped her legs around my waist, clinging to me like I was her everything. And maybe I was. It broke my fucking heart and something in me snapped.

With our mouths fused together, her tongue hypnotically rubbing against mine, I found my hands unbuttoning her pants. Rather than stop me, McKenna's hips pushed forward, her body eager for friction.

I needed her just as badly as she needed me. We were two lost souls fighting to cling to something real. But our first time shouldn't be like this – so desperate and full of anguish, mouths seeking, hands grasping, clutching for something to hold on to. We were a tangle of limbs and hands groping until each of us had shed the other of our clothes. I lifted a fully nude McKenna, strode with her across the room and lay us back against my bed. She straddled me and remained motionless for several seconds. The dim light in my room bathed her skin a faint golden glow. She'd never looked more beautiful to me than in that moment.

Pulling away from her mouth, I cupped her face in my hands. Hazy blue eyes slowly blinked open to meet mine. 'Not like this, not for your first time,' I breathed, my heart pounding.

'But this is how I need it. Make me forget everything else,' she whispered.

I wanted her to know only my name, to know it was me inside her, but she deserved to be loved, cherished, and I had fuck-all of a clue how to do that properly. I only knew the physical aspects – I dealt in pleasure and orgasms and how many condom wrappers were on the floor the next morning. But real intimacy, taking care of all a woman's needs – let alone a woman as complex as McKenna? It was a sure shot at failure.

But right then, in that moment, McKenna was just a girl looking for closeness any way she could get it. If that ended with me inside her, so be it. It was the only way I knew. And it seemed neither of us was capable of waiting anymore.

She was giving herself to me, despite knowing what I was. The most beautiful gift she had to offer was mine. Feeling her damp heat against my belly where she sat, and my erection brushing against her ass, desire rocketed through me.

Everything in me wanted to take control, to lift her hips and position her so she could slide down on me, but I knew if I did that, I'd hurt her. And since that wasn't in the cards, I hauled her off me, forcing her to lie on her back.

Coils of desire raced through my bloodstream, and I had to physically force myself to go slow. I kissed McKenna, long and deep, claiming her with my mouth. Never had I spent so much time just kissing, but with her, I found it strangely satisfying and hard to stop. When she was squirming beneath me on the bed, I dropped to my knees on the floor between her legs, taking her ankles in my hands and planting her feet on the bed so that she was wide open for me. McKenna's head lifted from the pillow and she looked at me, poised above her with wide set eyes. With my gaze locked on hers, I lowered my mouth to the juncture between her thighs and inhaled. McKenna flinched, her belly dipping as she sucked in a breath. She needed to understand that I loved the feminine scent of her arousal. That sweet fragrance made me lose all sense of right and wrong, all rational thought. Parting her glistening pink flesh, I swirled my tongue over her clit until a sob broke from her lips. Her entire body trembled, begging for release, while I ruthlessly licked against her.

Her orgasm hit me like a sucker punch to the gut. I was becoming addicted to giving pleasure rather than taking it. Emotions tore through me and I took a moment, sitting back on my heels and wondering how it was this beautiful woman I'd only known a short time had completely undone me.

'Knox,' she whimpered, reaching for me.

I crawled up onto the bed with her and McKenna immediately took my cock in her hands, rubbing and stroking just like I'd shown her. A dark hunger simmered inside me, pooling at the base of my spine, the need to be inside her overtaking me. I reached for a condom and rolled it down my length while McKenna watched and chewed on her lip. Hesitation surged inside me. Was I doing the right thing?

'Are you sure you're ready?'

Her hand curled around my eager cock, as if to feel the latex sheathing me. Every moment with her was a new awakening. It kept me grounded and in the moment like never before. 'I want you.' She pressed her lips to my throat, her hot breath rushing over my skin in the most reassuring way. She wanted this. Me. Even with all my shortcomings, she was choosing me.

And for the night, I was hers. Body and soul.

McKenna

After putting on the condom, Knox lay down beside me so we were facing each other on the bed. I rested my head on his arm and his other hand was between us, positioning his hard length against me.

Lying side by side like this wasn't the position I imagined. 'What are you doing?' I asked.

'I want to hold you. Is this okay?'

'Yeah, but it's just....'

'This isn't how you pictured it going?' he asked.

'No. I thought you'd be on top.' I remembered my embarrassing lecture to Luke about how to ensure a girl's first time was special. It showed how little I knew. I guess I never thought my first time would be with Knox, looking deep into his eyes. It sent a warm ripple of pleasure through me.

'We'll get there, but for your first time, me on top doesn't allow you to control the speed, angle, or depth, so I thought this might work better. I want you to be comfortable.'

I relaxed my head against the pillow. I was comfortable. I was lying on my side facing Knox and we were snuggled close. I could feel his warmth all around me and his scent sending me into my happy place. But warning bells were going off in my mind. Knowing Knox had a dominating side...I didn't want him softening this experience for me. I wanted to know he was right here with me, fifty-fifty, enjoying every moment, not sacrificing himself for something he thought I wanted. 'But I thought you liked taking control, I want to be sure you're....'

His lips against mine stopped me mid-rant. 'Not for your first time. This is about you.' He leaned forward and pressed another kiss to my lips, softer this time. 'Just try and relax, okay?'

I nodded and watched him.

He pressed the tip of himself against my opening. I tried to relax my muscles like he'd told me, but my body was anything buy welcoming to the blunt head of him. Lifting my top leg so I was spread apart, Knox cradled my calf in his big palm. I felt more exposed in this position, but when Knox's mouth went to my throat and began lightly nibbling me there, I forgot all about that.

He pressed his hips closer to mine again and I felt the very tip of him push inside me. Knox released a hiss through his teeth and pulled back. It wasn't working.

Dropping a kiss to my forehead, he looked deep into my eyes. 'Do you want some extra lubrication?'

'Whatever you want,' I murmured, hoping I wasn't doing something wrong.

His thumb stroked my cheek as he gazed down at me. 'I like it tight, I just don't want to hurt you.'

I was prepared for a little discomfort. 'It's okay. I'm fine.' I was a mess of nerves and my inner muscles trembled in anticipation, but I wanted this. I wanted him. Knox better not back out on me now. I couldn't have another failed attempt at losing my virginity. Using his hand to guide himself, Knox pressed harder, penetrating me, stealing the oxygen from my lungs, waking me up from the inside out. With his eyes locked on mine, he thrust deeper, several more inches slicing me open. My mouth dropped open in a silent scream.

With my body stretched to accommodate him, Knox moved slowly, using long measured strokes that I felt deep inside me – in a place no one had ever touched me before. But what I really savored was the look in his eyes. The way he was looking at me made my heart race and my body respond despite the pain. He was a man in need, dark hunger reflected back at me in his features. A warm shiver raced along my body.

I felt stretched to capacity, the sensation entirely new and slightly painful, but in the best possible way. Still, I didn't like the idea that Knox was holding back. I wanted to show him that I wasn't afraid of his dark side, that I could take whatever he wanted to give. Wrapping my legs around his back, I urged him closer. He released a guttural groan and buried his face against my neck. 'More, Knox,' I murmured. He obeyed, his hips slamming into me, forcing a cry to rip from my throat.

Knox

I worried for a moment that my weight was crushing her, but when McKenna's legs wound around my back, I lost all sense of rational thought. She squirmed beneath me, begging for more, and unrestrained need raced through my veins. Done holding back, I pounded into her tight channel without mercy. She cried out, all her muscles tightening around me.

A pang of guilt sucker punched me in the gut. I should be gentle with her, but that wasn't my style and I let my raw need to consume her overtake me. 'Are you okay?'

'Yeah,' she exhaled against my mouth, and I kissed her deeply, relief washing through me.

This might not have been my first time, but nothing about this was familiar to me. Sharing this with her meant something. It wasn't like all the other times when my mind shut down and I lost myself to the numbness of pleasure. I was aware of everything. Every heartbeat, every cry of pleasure, her hot breath rushing over my skin, the pull of her warm channel hugging me. She was intoxicating in the most sobering way.

I knew I was getting close, and since there was no way I was going off before her, I used the pad of my index finger to circle her clit and bent forward to kiss her breasts, latching onto one of her nipples and grazing it lightly with my teeth. McKenna shuddered in my arms, crying out in pleasure rather than pain this time. I pumped into her with long, measured strokes, continuing to pleasure her, and soon felt her body clench around mine with her climax. I held her while little tremors passed through her body, slowing my pace to allow her to enjoy every pulse and sensation. That certainly hadn't happened the last time I was with a virgin. I remember her begging me to just finish and the blood stains on her sheets when we were done. Back then I'd been in high school, though, and not nearly as skilled and unfortunately not as in-tune with a woman's pleasure. But with McKenna, that wasn't an option. I was tuned in to her every breath.

Moments later, I lost myself inside her, gripping her ass and letting her milk every last drop of fluid from my body. I clung to her long after, each of us unwilling to let the other go.

Sex had never been like that before. I would have been up and out the door the minute I got off. With McKenna, I reluctant to let her go even to remove the condom.

'Did I hurt you?' I asked.

She shook her head, curling against me.

She was so quiet, I worried I'd done something wrong and guilt churned inside me. 'How do you feel?'

'Happy,' she answered.

Releasing a sigh, I pulled her into my arms, drawing her even closer. 'Not too sore?'

'No, I don't think so.'

Relief washed over me. I knew I should apologize, I was too rough with her, but it was who I was, and if she wasn't complaining, then neither was I.

'Was everything okay for you?' she whispered.

I tipped her chin up to meet my eyes. 'That's what you're worried about? That I didn't enjoy myself?' I fought back a smile while she nodded up at me. 'It was perfect.' I pressed a tender kiss to her mouth, hoping that quieted all her fears about not measuring up. There was nothing to measure up to, with McKenna occupying all of my brain space I couldn't have recalled a previous partner if I tried.

We lay together as the room grew dark around us. Never in my life had I savored a quiet moment quite like this one. McKenna's head rested on my shoulder, her tangled hair splayed on the pillow between us, and her warm, soft body molded to mine. A monogamous healthy sexual relationship was completely foreign to me. And knowing this beautiful, sweet girl trusted me made my heart beat erratically. She believed in me when no one else did. She saw the man I hoped I could become.

My brothers would be home soon and I knew we needed to get up and get dressed, I just didn't want to. 'Are you hungry?' I asked finally. We'd skipped dinner and gone straight for dessert. The least I could do now was feed her.

'Why, are you going to cook for me?' The hint of a smile tugged at her mouth.

'Of course. Come on.' I urged her from our warm little nest and we dressed and headed downstairs.

Just as we were finishing a casual dinner of soup and sandwiches, I heard the front door swing open, followed by the sound of voices. The guys were home. I sent McKenna into the living room to relax while I cleaned up. After greeting her, Jaxon and Luke wandered into the kitchen.

'How was it?' I asked, adding the bowls and spoons to the dishwasher.

'Good, Tucker had fun, but we had to duck out the back way at the end because we ran into an old fling of mine,' Jaxon said.

Just great. I didn't want Tucker around Jax's booty-call drama.

'What's wrong with McKenna?' Luke asked, helping himself to the half-sandwich McKenna had left uneaten on her plate.

'What do you mean?'

'She winced when she sat down on the couch like she was in pain or something and her hair is all messy and out of place. She have a bad day at work or something?'

Shit. Jaxon's knowing gaze met mine and he shook his head. 'Something like that,' I bit out, my tone harsher than I intended.

'We should do something nice for her,' Luke said, oblivious to the silent exchange happening between me and Jax.

'Yeah, good idea.' I rubbed the back of my neck, completely at a loss.

'Maybe we could make her dessert or something,' Luke said, rummaging through the cabinets. 'What does she like?'

'No clue.' I wasn't winning boyfriend of the year – that was certain. And the way Jax was looking at me made me feel like the world's biggest asshole. I needed to fix this, to take care of my girl. 'I have another idea.'

After giving my orders to Jaxon and Luke, they headed up the stairs. Next I needed Tucker to go hunting through the cabinets in search of my next ingredient. 'Tuck,' I urged him from McKenna's lap. 'Come here, bud.'

He followed me up the stairs while McKenna watched curiously after us.

We met the guys in the second floor bathroom where Jaxon was gathering up mounds of dirty clothes from the floor and overflowing hamper and Luke was kneeling beside the bath tub, giving it a long overdue scrub down. Seeing that everything was underway, I sent Tucker on his task, searching the hall closet for some type of body wash that could double as bubble bath while I headed upstairs to gather a few candles I knew I had stashed in a drawer in case of power outages.

I met Jaxon in the hallway. 'Everything cleaned up in there?'

'It's getting there. Something happen tonight?' he asked, his eyes narrowed and locked on mine. For all the times I'd given him shit for his antics with girls, I knew his scowl was my payback.

'Nope.'

'Liar,' he muttered under his breath.

I wanted to tell him I would fix this and make things right, instead I released a deep sigh and went to finish the final details for McKenna's surprise. I might not be able to afford to buy her gifts or give her fancy things, but I hoped this small gesture would show her that I cared and that I was trying.

I considered running down to the corner store and picking up a bottle of wine or something until I remembered that the last time McKenna had drank she'd practically tried to jump me. No sense in encouraging that. She'd had enough for one night.

Instead, I had Tucker make her a cup of chocolate milk, which he brought up in one of our mother's china teacups.

Once everything was ready, I led a suspicious McKenna up the stairs by her hand. 'What are you guys up to?' she asked.

I stopped at the threshold to the bathroom and turned her by the shoulders. When she saw the three boys and behind them the tub filled with bubbles, the edges lined with white candles, she sucked in a breath. Luke switched off the lights and Tucker, impossible not to love, thrust his arms out to his sides and shouted, 'Surprise!'

'What's all this?'

'It's for you, angel,' I whispered, leaning in close to kiss her temple. 'The guys helped me. We thought you could use some relaxation.'

McKenna silently gripped my hand in a wordless thank you. The expression on her face told me it had been a long time since anyone had done something nice for her. She served others all day long, and the unshed tears simmered in her blue eyes as she struggled to believe she was worth such care and attention.

'Clear out, guys.'

McKenna stopped them on their way out, planting a kiss on each of their cheeks. 'Thank you.' Tucker threw his arms around her middle, squeezing her tightly.

When the door closed us in, I spun her to face me. Lazy steam vapors drifted up around us and the low flickering light of the candles gave everything a sense of calm. I pressed a kiss to her waiting mouth. 'You lied to me. You're sore, aren't you?'

'Is that what the bath's for?'

I didn't answer, I just kissed her again. 'There are fresh towels in the cabinet under the sink. I'll meet you upstairs when you're through.'

She nodded and took my face in both her hands, bringing her mouth close to mine. 'Thank you.'

The warm whisper of breath on my skin was the only thanks I needed. 'Enjoy, angel. Oh, and Tucker brought you chocolate milk.' I nodded towards the cup on the counter beside the sink.

'I like the pink teacup. Nice touch.' She grinned.

'It was our mom's favorite.' I left her with a smile blossoming on her lips. 'Take your time.'

Chapter Fourteen

McKenna

After my bath I found Knox in bed, half asleep. I dropped my towel and climbed in beside him, curling my naked body around his. 'Hi,' I whispered, kissing the spot behind his ear.

'Feel better?' he asked.

I nodded, rubbing my lips against his neck. 'Yes. That was lovely.' I hadn't soaked in a hot bath like that in ages. And he was right, I had been sore. The warm water had soothed most of the lingering ache reminding me of where he'd been, deep within me. And the bubbles made from Knox's manly-scented body wash had made the experience that much better. I felt closer to him. Surrounded by him. I hadn't wanted to get out – and didn't until the water had started to turn cold.

I wished I could put into words what tonight had meant to me. Our lovemaking, him taking care of me like that...I'd never experienced anything like it. I was falling for this man, body, heart, and soul. Part of that scared me, but mostly I felt happy and safe. 'Thank you, Knox.'

'You're welcome, angel,' he murmured.

'I love you.' I hadn't planned on telling him – I had barely let myself think those three dangerous words, but before I could even process what I was doing, they were out of my mouth and lingering in the air between us. My heart pounded unsteadily and the calmness I'd found vanished in an instant.

Several agonizing moments of silence passed between us. I knew he'd heard me. I knew he was still awake. I also knew I probably just triggered every defense mechanism Knox had put in place. Dread churned in my stomach, twisting it into a painful knot. I was dying to know what he was thinking. Surely he felt the pounding of my heart against his back, the faint sweat breaking out over my skin. Knox gave my hand a careful squeeze, but said nothing.

The next morning, seated behind my desk at group, the weight of what I'd done came crashing down on me the moment Knox strolled into the room looking happy and carefree.

I'd lost my virginity last night to a man who was in sexual addiction recovery. I could lose my counseling license. I could lose everything I'd worked hard for – and for what? While I was falling deeper and deeper, I had no idea what it would lead to. Did Knox even love me? He'd told me time and again he wasn't capable of love. I was finally starting to see the ramifications of that. The risks I was taking for him could all be for nothing. My chest felt tight as I watched him take a seat across the room without so much as acknowledging me.

That week's group was the most awkward experience of my life. Each member shared the number of days since their last sexual encounter and when Knox said one – my cheeks flamed as memories of me unabashedly grinding against him in his bed last night came flooding back. I didn't know how to reconcile these two halves of myself – the counselor helping him heal and the girl who wanted to fall into his arms and give in to the pleasure of the moment.

It seemed like I'd lived a lifetime of new experiences since I'd first watched him saunter through that door just a few short months ago. So much had changed and yet nothing really had. I had Knox in my life now – but the threat of his past still threatened our future, I still had Brian playing the overprotective and slightly possessive big brother, and I'd yet to face my own past. Dread churned inside me. I had a strange feeling everything I held dear was about to collide.

There were times I thought we could really do this – forge a real relationship built on honesty and trust. Like when I'd been neck deep in bubbles last night, feeling pampered and cherished. Other times, like this moment sitting in sex addicts anonymous, or when Knox hadn't returned my *I love you* I realized I was living in a fantasy land and that this relationship had far more complications than I gave it credit for.

As the weeks passed, I became less and less sure about what I was doing. My life was spinning out of control further by the day. It made me miss my mother and her pragmatic advice more than ever. I was falling deeper and deeper for a man with an inability to love me back and my weekly group sessions were becoming something I dreaded. They were heavy and intense and I felt like a complete hypocrite.

Everything I did felt like a burden I could just barely carry the weight of and by the end of the day, I collapsed heavily into bed alone, my chest an aching hole. I thought I could do it, be with Knox on his terms, wait for him to come around and continue leading SAA, but I was quickly beginning to realize it was too much for me. I was emotionally invested in both – loving Knox and helping with his recovery – and I didn't even know where we stood.

I'd kept myself busy with work and volunteering in an attempt to give him a bit of space. I'd met up with Amanda a few times and we'd been scouring resale shops for pink baby clothes. Even Knox's neighbor Nikki had helped out – sending a big bag of Bailee's old clothes home with me for Amanda. But none of my distractions helped. I was consumed by my growing love for Knox and the undeniable guilt about the relationship we were carrying on.

Knox was picking me up from my apartment tonight since he'd become increasingly difficult about me taking the bus. I had my backpack slung over my shoulder with pajamas, a few toiletries, and clothes for tomorrow since heaven forbid I leave a few things over at his place. I didn't want to freak him out. I was sharing his bed, but I knew I wasn't occupying the space I really wanted to – his heart.

Brian watched me from the corner of his eye, disapproval written all over his face.

'I'll see you tomorrow,' I murmured, stuffing my keys in my coat pocket.

'That lawyer called again.'

Crap. I chewed on my lip, avoiding his eyes.

'You ever gonna deal with that?' he asked.

Not if I don't have to. 'I will, Bri. Soon,' I promised. Spotting the headlights of Knox's Jeep from the front window, I headed out the door.

'Hi,' I murmured, climbing inside the darkened interior of the Jeep. The scent of warm leather and Knox's unique masculine scent of sandalwood washed over me and calmed me in an instant. Maybe things would all work out. I just needed to have patience.

'Hi, beautiful.' He kissed my forehead before pulling out onto the road. 'The guys have missed you.'

Reading between the lines, I wondered if he had missed me and that was his way of letting me know. I craved his affection, craved honesty and realness from him, but I sensed he was still holding himself back from me. 'I missed them, too.'

When we arrived home I was accosted by Tucker, who seemed to grow an inch every time I saw him. 'Hey buddy.' I rumpled his hair. 'How's school?'

'Good. Will you read to me tonight?'

'Sure.' Casting a quick glance at Knox, I let Tucker take my hand and pull me upstairs to his bedroom.

After three books and a sleepy goodnight hug, I pulled the blankets up around Tucker and met Knox in his attic bedroom. He was sprawled out across his bed with his sketchbook balanced on his chest. 'Tucker get settled in okay?'

I nodded. 'Yeah, he's out cold.'

He studied me for a second, watching the way I stood in the center of his bedroom, my eyes sweeping over the room. 'What's on your mind?' he asked, patting the bed bedside him.

Take your pick. That letter I'd yet to open from the lawyer in Indiana concerning my parents' estate, Knox's failure to fully commit, my guilt over sleeping with a sex addict in recovery, or Brian's recent admission that he wanted to be with me. I felt dizzy just thinking about it all.

I couldn't dump all of that on Knox right now. Releasing a heavy sigh, I decided to tell him the least painful part. 'Brian asked a few weeks ago if he had a shot with me. He said it's what my parents would have wanted.'

'And what did you say?' His face was impassive, but I hoped that maybe this would push him into action. I wasn't going to be happy with our arrangement forever. I wanted a real commitment, love, a relationship that I knew could eventually grow into something more.

'I couldn't say anything. My parents loved him.'

'I see.' I wondered if that was a twinge of disappointment or fear that flashed in his chocolate brown eyes. Before I could decide, his expression had turned stoic.

With Knox's cool demeanor – he was neither pushing me away, nor drawing me closer. I wondered if it was time to go back to Indiana and deal with my past once and for all.

'I don't know what this is, but you know how I feel about you, right?' I asked.

He nodded, but gave me no indication he shared those feelings. I wanted to push him for answers – to ask him to explain – but I feared hearing his answer, so instead I sat on his bed, quietly picking at the hem of my sweater.

'Tell me what else is on your mind. There's something more than just Brian's infatuation bugging you.'

'This is too much for me. I thought I could do it – be with you and lead SAA, but I can't.' The heavy sigh weighing on my chest ripped free. 'I'm emotionally invested in both and I don't even know where we stand.'

'That's fair,' he said quietly, looking down at his sketchbook.

I hated how calm and cool he was about it all. What did he mean? What was happening to us? Whoever said sex changed everything between a man and a woman was right.

'I need to go back to Indiana. There's something I need to take care of. And I'm going to ask Brian to come with me.'

He nodded. Piercing brown eyes gazed up at me, making my chest ache. 'When are you leaving?'

I shrugged. I hadn't talked to Bri yet – with this being a spur of the moment decision and all. 'Probably around the holidays. I know his mom will want to see me.' With Christmas just a week away, it made sense.

'You're still staying over tonight, right?'

'Do you want me to?'

'Of course I do. I'll always want you here, McKenna.' His voice was so sincere and the look in his eyes was genuine, but I still felt like something was missing. I'd gotten him to open up and I'd convinced him to let me share his bed, but I hadn't gotten what I really wanted – the real Knox, unedited and genuine. He was still holding part of himself back and that hurt more than I ever thought it would.

I headed into the bathroom with my backpack, planning to brush my teeth and change clothes. Instead, I sank down on the toilet lid and silently cried.

After I'd dried my tears, I cleaned myself up and emerged from the bathroom a short time later. I found Knox waiting for me in bed with just the soft glow of his bedside lamp to guide my way. I crawled into bed beside a man who owned my heart and made me dizzy with desire, yet offered me so little in return. Maybe this was some type of self-punishment I was putting myself through. Wouldn't Brian be the easier choice? He'd love me unconditionally and without all this worry that kept my stomach in knots. But maybe that was just it. Anything worth having wasn't going to come easily. I knew without a shadow of a doubt I'd fallen in love with Knox, and I hoped me heading home to Indiana would give him some time to think about what he wanted.

Chapter Fifteen

Knox

I was losing her. And that couldn't happen. With desperation, I dragged her across the bed and positioned her beneath me, kissing her hard until I felt her respond, her tongue sliding against mine, her legs parting to let me press closer. I hated that this felt like goodbye and I was using the only coping mechanism I had – sex. But I couldn't open myself up for love again and be crushed in the process. This was what I had to offer and while I wondered if McKenna could accept that, her body seemed to be on board.

Her dancing around her talk with Brian and taking off for home meant one thing. She was keeping her options open just in case I fucked up again. She would need someone to fall back on, and Brian was her backup plan. I couldn't fuck up again or I'd send her straight into his arms for comfort. The realization terrified me. Because while I might be holding it all together right now, there were no guarantees that I'd remain on this path. And if McKenna was set on going home, I would show her exactly what she'd be missing.

I might not be able to tell her I loved her, but I could make her feel good. Moving from her eager mouth to her throat, my lips pressed against her pulse point, feeling her heart riot in response. Planting damp kisses and peppering her with gentle bites, I worked my way lower, removing her T-shirt to reveal her ample chest. I wasn't capable of going slow just now and McKenna's writhing, whimpering responses told me she was okay with that. I nibbled at the skin between her breasts, pushing them together and feasting on them greedily. I loved her tits. The way they rose and fell dramatically with her breaths, the moans that would escape her when I flicked my tongue across their peaks…she made me rock hard from her taste and scent alone, and then add in the sounds she made and I was done.

Pushing her pajama bottoms and panties down her legs, I positioned myself on top of her. I was rougher, more demanding than last time and I wasn't sure if it was my fear taking over or just that the need for her was consuming me from the inside out. Finding her wet and ready, I sheathed myself in a condom and took her roughly, plunging into her again and again until I felt her give way and I was buried to the hilt.

I pressed my face into her neck, needing to breath in her scent, needing to know it was just her and me. 'Christ, angel, you feel like a hot little sleeve squeezing me.'

'Knox….' She moaned out my name long and low and tightened her grip around me. Her nails scratched into my shoulders, but I appreciated the pain. That way I knew this moment with her was real. I pounded into her, again and again, taking from her. Taking every bit of emotion she made me feel and using it as fuel.

She had embedded herself into my life, made me need her. I'd never needed a woman the way I needed McKenna. Her bright smile. Her giving nature. The sound of her laughter, the curse words she made up when she was playing video games with my brothers. She held complete power over me and that scared the shit out of me. I hated the idea of letting her go away with Brian, but saw no other choice.

Sex used to make me feel in control, but this was anything but controlled and organized. McKenna tore through all my layers, refusing to submit. She was an active participant, encouraging, panting, angling our bodies to drive me deeper, and hell if I wanted to stop her.

Soon I was fighting off the inevitable climax I could feel building at the base of my spine and I focused on bringing McKenna to the edge. I wanted her helpless and sobbing my name. Spreading her knees wider, I slowed my pace, dragging my length in and out of her slowly while simultaneously rubbing her clit over and over with the slick juices between us. Her eyes slammed closed and she groaned.

'Open them, angel.'

Hazy blue eyes struggled to focus on mine and I continued rocking into her at my languid pace until she found my gaze.

'Be a good girl and don't come until I do.'

Her eyes widened and she let out a soft whimper. I pumped into her hard and fast, slamming my cock into her warmth until my balls tightened against my body and pleasure was ricocheting through my bloodstream. I pulled out of her at the last moment, tearing off the condom and coming all over her tight little pussy. I marked her swollen pink flesh, using my cock to rub my semen against her clit. McKenna moaned out loud, watching as I pleasured her.

I brought her fingertips to her belly where some of my fluid remained. 'Touch your nipples.'

She obeyed, taking her breasts in her hands and using the moisture to rub her nipples. Watching her touch her breasts while I pleasured her was the most erotic sight. I rubbed her clit with the head of my cock, using the stimulation to bring her to orgasm. 'Come for me, angel.'

Her climax hit her hard. Her hips bucked off the bed and her nails bit into my thighs as tremors passed through her shuddering form.

We lay together for a long while, our bodies slick with sweat and sex, but neither of us caring. My cock softened and the evidence of our lovemaking dried long before I was ready to move. This felt like goodbye and I hated the idea of letting her go off alone and deal with her past, including whatever it was she needed to explore with Brian. I climbed from bed and while the water heated for the shower, I delivered a damp cloth to McKenna to clean to herself. Neither of us spoke a single word. Shit, we even avoided eye contact while we cleaned ourselves up and dressed for bed, crawling between the sheets a short while later. I wasn't sure what had changed, but I knew something had. McKenna had a choice to make on her trip home and I had to decide – if she came back to me – how to fully let her in.

Chapter Sixteen

McKenna

The events of last night had me reeling and the harsh light of morning did nothing to bring clarity. When I'd told Knox about Brian's advances and that I needed to go home, he'd been so indifferent. But then he'd taken me to his bed – our lovemaking rough and passionate. I couldn't help but wonder if that was his way of letting me go.

Last night had been so intense, so unexpected. Feeling him mark me with his hot semen made me crave him even more. Everything about Knox was addicting – from the way he took charge of my body and my pleasure to the way he commanded my heart.

I climbed from bed while he slept, hauling my backpack to the bathroom to wash up and change. When I returned to his bedroom, I wondered how I would wake him, how I could possibly say goodbye, but the bed was now empty. The messy blankets were the only evidence of our night spent together. But finding him missing wasn't what stopped me dead in my tracks. On the window beside his bed I saw three little words written with a fingertip on the frosty pane of glass. *I love you.*

Knox has left me a message, something he wasn't capable of telling me out loud.

I sunk down on the mattress, trying to process what this meant – why he'd left this for me to see and then fled the room. I wanted to run down the stairs, find him, and throw myself into his arms. But as I sat there staring at the words fading into the glass, I started to become angry.

I'd given him my virginity, my complete trust, I'd told him I loved him. I'd cared for him and his brothers when they were sick and I'd risked my entire career. And for what? A man who seemed so indifferent to me leaving? Who didn't even possess the courage to say back to me what I'd already told him weeks ago?

Feeling crushed, I glanced up one last time, and saw the words had faded into nothing. They were gone. Not even a trace remained. If Knox had really wanted me to see this…why would he have written it somewhere so fleeting?

I grabbed my backpack and headed downstairs. All four of the Bauer boys were in the kitchen, fixing breakfast while Knox fiddled with the coffee pot. He took his time, adding the filter and coffee to the machine, then crossing the room to add water to the carafe. Was he avoiding me?

'I'm gonna head out. Have a good day at school, boys.' Three sets of warm brown eyes turned to mine while Knox focused on his task with a deep crease etched across his forehead. 'Bye, Knox.' I forced the words from my mouth when all I wanted to do was go to him.

'Bye, McKenna,' he said softly, refusing to even glance my way.

Okay, then. I wouldn't build up our relationship in my mind into something it wasn't. He wasn't ready and only time would tell if he ever would be.

Chapter Seventeen

McKenna

'You about ready, McKenna?' Brian called from the living room several days later.

'Just about. My suitcase weighs a metric ton!' I tugged the unwieldy thing unsuccessfully across my room. I knew he wanted to be on the road early this morning and the main hold up was me.

'Here. Let me get it.' Brian easily lifted the suitcase from the floor and towed it to the foyer. 'Geez, you pack enough?' He chuckled.

Seriously, that bag had to weigh fifty pounds. But I didn't know how long I'd be gone. This time I was going to take care of my parents' matters once and for all. No more having my past hanging over my head. When I came back to Chicago, it would be with all the skeletons in my closet cleared out so I could finally move forward. At least that was my goal.

Being back in my small home town and back in the guest room at Brian's parents' house felt strange. I expected it to feel safe and comfortable, but it was anything but. I felt oddly out of place, like I was trying to squeeze myself into a spot I no longer fit. And if I had to hear Brian's mom Patty ask me one more time how I was doing or tell me that I'd gotten too thin, I was going to scream.

But it was Christmas Eve, so I was trying to be calm and put on my happy face for the sake of the holidays.

I was getting ready for the annual Christmas party Brian's family threw every year when I heard a knock at the bedroom door. Glancing down at my robe covered body, I quickly made sure all the important stuff was covered, then answered the door. 'Hi, Bri.'

He was dressed in khakis and the God-awful Christmas sweater his mom had made for him when he was in high school. It looked itchy and uncomfortable – not to mention hilarious. He was a grown man with red and green reindeer dancing across his chest and stomach.

'Don't say anything,' he warned me, fighting off a smile.

I patted his shoulder. 'You're a good son.'

'Consider yourself lucky she didn't make you one of these things. When I told her you were coming home, there was talk of patchwork poinsettias in gold and red.'

'Wow, I guess I dodged a bullet.' It was nice – whatever this was – happening between Brian and me. It felt like old times.

'You sure you're okay with tonight?'

'Yeah, why wouldn't I be?'

He shrugged. 'There'll be a lot of people you haven't seen in a while. If that's going to make you uncomfortable, you don't have to come.'

Releasing a heavy sigh, I considered my options. Though I wasn't particularly excited about the party, sitting alone in my room sounded even more miserable. 'And what would I do instead, hide out up here?'

'No. You and I would go out and do our own thing – catch a movie or something.'

His offer was sweet, but no, I could handle this. I leaned in and kissed his cheek. 'I'll be fine.'

He smiled at me, a genuine heart-warming smile that put me at ease. 'Okay. Choice is yours. If tonight gets to be too much, just say the word and we're gone.'

As nice as it was knowing I had options, I needed to do this – if only to prove to myself that I could. 'I'm good. Just don't leave me alone with Jimmy Shane. You remember how grabby he was in high school?'

'He tries to touch you and I can promise I'll remove every finger from his hand.' He grinned. 'Well, I just stopped by to see if you needed anything from the store…my mom's sending me out for more eggnog before the party starts.'

'Nope, I'm good. I just need to finish getting ready.'

'Okay, see you soon then.'

When a police officer stood at the front door an hour later, his face ashen and grim, my stomach plummeted to my toes. It was eerily similar to that fateful day two policemen had shown up at my door and told me about my parents. All those horrible feelings came rushing straight back. I gripped the arm of the man standing next to me, not caring in the slightest that it was Jimmy Shane.

I watched in slow motion as Brian's parents, Patty and Dave, stepped into the hallway with the cop. When Patty broke out in a loud sob and buried her face against her husband's chest, I crumpled into a ball, collapsing onto the floor. Something had happened to Brian.

The room around me spun, tilting and pitching violently. The police officer left, Dave got Patty settled on the couch, and then made some type of announcement. The blood rushing in my ears blocked out what was said. Or maybe I just wasn't ready to know yet. Party-goers began to filter out. I remained frozen to the spot I'd claimed on the living room carpet, too afraid to move, unable to think.

When Dave lifted me to my feet a short time later, I struggled to make sense of his words. The roads had been icy. Brian was in a car accident. He was at Mercy West in critical condition. He handed me my coat and was waiting for me to respond.

'Are you coming with us?'

Brian was alive? 'Of course.'

We piled into the car, my nerves completely shot. Even though Brian was alive, I couldn't let myself breathe just yet. My dad had survived his accident for two days in critical condition before the blood hemorrhage in his brain ended his life. And I knew Patty and Dave were probably thinking the same thing. They'd stayed by my side through it all, sleeping in hospital waiting rooms and eating out of vending machines right alongside me. It was only fitting that I be here now with them in their darkest hour. Hugging my arms around myself for warmth in the backseat, I watched as they held hands on the center console – gripping each other tightly. I felt scared and alone.

Brian looked worse than I expected. And even though I'd been down this road before, nothing could adequately prepare you to see someone you care about pale and broken in a hospital bed, punctured with tubes and hooked up to machines beeping about God knows what. But for his parents' sake, I tried to be the calm one and hold it together while they cried over his limp and battered body.

He had lacerations on his face and head from flying glass, a punctured lung when the airbag deployed after he'd struck the lamppost, a concussion and a leg broken in three spots. But he was stable and assuming he did well over the next couple days, he'd be downgraded from critical to serious condition. The doctors were taking every safety precaution, but believed Brian would pull through.

The next day was a blur – but in an all too familiar way. The constant worry and stress, the sterile hospital air, a stiff neck from sleeping in an uncomfortable chair, and the dark circles lining my eyes were all too familiar.

In the chaos of it all, I'd somehow forgotten it was Christmas Day. I thought of Knox and the boys and missed them with every ounce of my being. I wanted nothing more than to be wrapped up tight in Knox's strong arms and tucked safely away from all this heartache. But I supposed being near him brought a different kind of heartache. I wondered what they were doing today... if they had a Christmas tree in the living room with wrapped presents underneath, or if they were working together to make a big dinner later.

I looked up to see Dave dozing quietly in a chair beside Brian's bed and Patty flipping through a magazine for the twelfth time. 'I'm going to go make a quick phone call,' I whispered to Patty. 'You want another cup of coffee?'

'Sure, hon, that'd be great.'

It was all she'd eaten or drank since we'd arrived here yesterday.

Stepping into the hallway, I took a moment to gather myself. I had no idea what to expect calling Knox. We hadn't talked in eight long days. Not since he'd so thoroughly claimed my body and then let me walk away without a backward glance.

I leaned against the wall for support, drawing deep breaths as I dialed his number.

'McKenna....' he answered on the first ring.

The rough sound of his voice brought a thousand memories rushing back. 'Hi.'

'Are you still in Indiana?' he asked.

I swallowed the lump in my throat. 'Yeah.'

'What's wrong? Did something happen?'

I should have known he'd hear it in my voice. He knew me too well. 'Oh God, Knox....' Tears sprang to my eyes and the tightness in my chest threatened to close my throat. 'It's Brian...I don't know what to do....'

'Christ, what's he done now?' he barked.

'No, nothing...he was in a car accident. I'm at the hospital. I slept here last night with his parents.'

'You weren't in the car with him, were you?'

'No. I was at his parents' house when it happened.'

'Fuck,' he muttered under his breath. 'Is he okay?'

'I – I don't know yet.' My voice broke and I chocked on my words, tears freely streaming down both cheek. It was the first time I'd cried since I'd found out about the accident. I'd held it together in front of his parents and the parade of doctors and nurses, but somehow the comforting familiar sound of Knox's deep voice sent me over the edge.

Knox waited while I sobbed, fighting for breath, never once rushing me. 'He was banged up pretty bad, but they've repaired his lung and his leg, so as long as the concussion didn't do any damage, he should be okay.'

'Breathe for me, angel. It'll be okay.'

I drew a deep breath, struggling to regain my composure. The busy nurses and hospital staff shuffling past paid me little attention. Apparently a girl crying uncontrollably in the hallway was a normal occurrence. I forced myself to maintain my hard-won sense of self-control, focusing on the sound of Knox's steady breaths to calm me.

'I'm sorry….' I whispered.

'Don't apologize. Are you all right?'

'I think so. I just hate being back in this hospital, and I hate feeling so helpless. I mean, this is Bri…we've been inseparable since first grade.'

'Hang in there, okay?'

I nodded and then smiled, realizing he couldn't see me. 'I'll try.'

'So I know it's the wrong time to ask, but the guys miss you. Any idea when you'll be coming back?'

'No clue. I've taken a leave from work. I want to be here for Brian, ya know?' I had requested one because I wasn't sure how long all of this would take, and now with the accident, I was even less certain.

'Understood.'

Was that sadness in his voice? 'He was there for me when, you know, so I should be here for him and his parents.'

'Of course. I get it, McKenna. You guys have a past and he's been in an accident. It makes sense you'd want to be by his side.'

'Yeah.' I shuffled my feet, trying to think of something else to say. I wasn't done hearing his voice.

'Merry Christmas, angel,' he whispered.

I'd forgotten that was the reason I'd called in the first place. 'Merry Christmas,' I whispered back. 'What are you guys up to today?'

'Nikki and the baby came over for a little bit. Tucker had gotten Bailee a gift. And now we're getting ready to head out. We're actually going to the soup kitchen to volunteer. We're cooking Christmas dinner for those with nowhere else to go today.'

My throat felt tight again. 'Knox...that's amazing.'

'Yeah, well, there's this certain girl who sort of changed my way of thinking about things. Jax complained a little bit, but I think it'll be really good for the guys.'

'I'm proud of you.' I had to physically force myself not to say I love you. I loved him with my whole heart, but I couldn't stand the thought of being so vulnerable and hearing silence again. Little by little he was changing and growing into the man I always knew he could be. 'I guess I should go. Brian's mom is waiting on me.'

'Take care of yourself, McKenna.'

'Bye, Knox.'

I hung up the phone and cried like a baby.

When I'd finally composed myself, I ventured downstairs to the hospital cafeteria and got the cup of coffee I'd promised Patty. When I returned to Brian's room I found Patty sitting in the arm chair beside the bed, but Dave was gone.

'He went home to get a change of clothes for us. He'll be back in a little bit and you can borrow the car if you want to go home to shower or change,' she informed me.

'Okay, thanks.' A shower sounded heavenly, but I didn't want to leave on the chance that Brian woke up.

Patty hung her head in her hands, her expression pure agony. 'I just keep thinking what if I hadn't sent him out, I knew the roads were icy…all over a carton of eggnog….' Her voice broke as she sobbed into her hands.

'Patty….' I crossed the room and stood beside her, placing one hand on her shoulder. 'This isn't your fault. Accidents happen.' In that moment, my clarity couldn't have been more apparent if I'd been struck by lightning. Seeing Patty's anguish and guilt made me feel so foolish for holding onto my own guilt for all these years. My parents' accident wasn't my fault. What I'd said to her was true. Accidents happened. They happened to good people and sometimes no one was to blame. Though I supposed that wasn't entirely true. In my parents' case. The drunk driver who'd taken their lives was very much to blame. 'Shh, it's gonna be okay. Brian's gonna pull through.' I continued rubbing her back, soothing her as best as could, but inside, my thoughts were swirling. My realization changed everything. I felt freer and more aware in an instant – more grown up. Little by little, I felt the dark shame I stored inside me slipping away.

My adolescent mind at seventeen wasn't mature enough to handle their deaths. I'd needed someone to blame – and I'd punished myself. But the twenty-one year old me was seeing things clearly for the first time and the results were astounding. Despite the horrible circumstances of the moment, I felt more in control than ever. We would all be okay. Once Brian was healthy, I would go back to Chicago and try to fix things with Knox. We were grown up enough to have a conversation about the scary *L* word. He either loved me and wanted to be with me, or he didn't. And I would have to accept his decision and move forward with my life once and for all.

Chapter Eighteen

McKenna

As the days turned to weeks, Brian's recovery progressed quickly and I had no choice but to finally face my fears. I'd set up an appointment and visited the lawyer earlier that day. I was still trying to process the shocking truth of it all as I sat quietly at my parents' gravestones.

I'd known that between their insurance policies, pension plans, and the sale of our house I'd been left a significant chunk of money, I just hadn't expected it to affect me so much. It felt so final walking out of the lawyer's office with a large check in my hands. It was a life-changing amount of money and just as I was starting to get things figured out in my own head, I knew it was going to change everything. It would change where I lived, how Knox viewed me…even what I did for a living if I chose… and unease churned inside me. I wasn't good at change.

Knox and I continued talking every few days – surface level stuff – he'd fill me in on the boys and I'd give him Brian's progress report. We never talked about us. I never told him how I missed him with every ounce of my being, and he felt more distant than ever. As hard as it was to imagine, I wondered if he'd slipped back into his old ways.

I was planning to return to Chicago while Brian stayed behind for physical therapy for his leg. No longer living on a few dollars a day meant I could rent a car and drive myself home.

I huddled into my coat as the chilly air swirled loose strands of hair around my face. The bitter temperature and icy barren ground matched the somber tone of this reunion with my parents. I tucked my mitten-covered hands into my pockets as I filled them in on Brian. I talked out loud, the sound of my voice my only company. As I told them about the events of the past few weeks, I realized that my parents had liked Brian and viewed him as a good match for me because he'd always treated me well and protected me. Knox protected and took care of those he loved, too. And he made me happy. At the end of the day, my parents would have wanted me to be happy. It wasn't lost on me that my lack of attraction to Brian was because there was nothing to fix. He was a perfectly nice, well-adjusted man from a normal, nice family. But it didn't matter the reasons – the attraction wasn't there and it never would be. I had to believe my parents would have accepted that.

Knox had been right about one thing – one day I would forgive myself and move on. Today had proven I was capable of that, in small doses. But he'd been wrong about himself not fitting into my life. Being near Brian produced no spark, no electricity, and I missed the warmth that Knox created in me. I knew that by the end of this week, I'd be more than ready to get back. I was even considering changing up my punishing routine – volunteering fewer hours a week, taking more time to take care of myself and enjoy the little things in life. If I'd learned only one thing on this trip, it was that life was short and could be ripped from you at any moment.

I was also starting to feel guilty for not acknowledging his handwritten *I love you* message left on the window for me. He was still healing and that was his way of trying. I needed to acknowledge his efforts and progress, not act like a spoiled child who needed everything her way.

If my parents were really out there somewhere listening to this, I wanted to think they'd understand that Brian would always be a constant reminder of what I'd lost. Brian was my past. Knox was my future.

Digging my cell phone out of my coat pocket, I dialed Knox.

Chapter Nineteen

Knox

Seeing McKenna's name flash on my phone made me ridiculously fucking happy. I rounded the service counter at the hardware store where I was working and headed for the stockroom, tossing the pair of pliers I was supposed to be price checking onto a shelf. The customer would have to wait.

I ducked into the dusty stockroom and closed the door behind me. 'Hey, angel.'

'Hi,' she returned, her voice whisper-soft.

'Everything okay over there? Brian?' As much as saying his name grated against my nerves, the guy had gotten pretty messed up in that accident, so I didn't want to be a complete asshole and not ask how he was doing. Still, I'd be lying if I said it didn't make me insane with jealousy that McKenna had put her entire life on hold – put us on hold – to tend to him and stick by his side. I couldn't help but feel she'd chosen him over me.

I wished I'd had the balls that morning to take her in my arms and tell her I loved her. But instead I'd taken the pussy way out and scrawled it onto the window. There was a good chance she never even saw it. I sent her away into the arms of her very male best friend without even telling her how I felt. Basically I was a jackass.

'Brian's doing fine. I think he's annoyed at the slow pace of his recovery with his leg and his mom's constant hovering, but considering how things could have turned it, he's very lucky.'

'And how are you?'

She hesitated for several seconds before answering. 'I realized some things this week.'

'And what's that?' I wasn't religious, but I prayed to God it wasn't that she'd figured out Brian was the better choice for her and she was staying in Indiana.

'My parents' accident wasn't my fault. It was the damn reckless, irresponsible drunk driver.' Her voice wavered ever-so-slightly and she took a moment to compose herself. 'I was talking to Brian's mom Patty after the accident and it all just hit me. My actions that morning may not have made a difference in the outcome. And for years I thought maybe I should have been with them. But I see now that I wasn't meant to go then. I'm here for a reason. I'm here to do good in the world.'

'That's great to hear, angel. And you're right. You had nothing to do with the accident.'

'I know that now. I can't image how someone could be so selfish, so negligent. I will never forgive the man who did this. I have zero tolerance for drunk drivers.'

I was happy to hear her channel her anger into the right place – McKenna wasn't responsible for her parents' deaths. The man behind the wheel was. But cold dread slithered down my spine realizing, I'd never told McKenna about my own drunk driving arrest. Would it be a deal breaker for me and her?

'I'm going to be coming home soon,' she continued.

'Can I see you when you get home?'

'Yeah, and there's something I have to tell you when I get back.'

'Something good or something bad?' I asked.

'Um, just something…different. About my life. I finally met with my parents' lawyer.'

'Okay.' I had no clue where this was heading, but I'd follow her lead on this one. 'See you soon, then?'

'Yeah. Goodbye, Knox.'

'Bye.'

Chapter Twenty

Knox

'Do you want to talk about it or are you going to keep moping around here like someone kicked you in the balls?' Jaxon asked, glancing up from the TV.

'Are you going to watch the game or are we going to pretend this is Oprah?' I asked.

He smirked. 'Fine. But the guys know something's up. You're not yourself. You've been acting like a dick ever since McKenna took off. Care to tell me what's really going on?'

The feeling that I'd lost McKenna churned in my gut. I couldn't sleep. Food didn't taste right and when I tried to drink to numb the pain, I couldn't even catch a buzz. Luke had taken Tucker to the public library, so it was just me and Jaxon at home today. 'I talked to McKenna. She's coming home soon.'

'That's a good thing, right?'

'Yeah, I mean, I think so. But she said we have to talk when she gets back. I think she's had some sort of realization about her past and finally accepted that her parents were killed by a drunk driver and not because of anything she did.'

'And?' Jax drew out the word.

Apparently I needed to spell it out for him. 'And she doesn't know I was arrested for drunk driving and that my sentence was what brought me into her class in the first place.' Not mentioning it at the time was an omission – it just never really came up, but keeping it from her now felt like a deceitful lie.

'Shit. That sucks.'

I blew out a frustrated breath. 'Tell me about it.'

Jax flipped the channel on the TV. 'That's why I don't do love. As soon as you let your walls down, shit falls apart and then you're the one sitting there feeling like shit. It's easier to hit it and quit it.'

'Nice, Jaxon.'

He shrugged. 'It's just the truth and you know it. You lived that way for years.'

I couldn't argue; he knew my history too well. 'Well, sometimes feeling something is a good thing. It reminds us that we're still human.' I'd rather be having no sex with McKenna than be sleeping with a bunch of random girls, but I knew nothing I said would get through to him. He'd have to figure all this out on his own one day, too.

Jaxon rose from the couch and handed me the remote. 'I know I'm not good at this shit, but you know you have to talk to her, right?'

I nodded. 'Yeah. Thanks, bro.'

I knew I needed to talk to her, but I wasn't sure that would make a difference. With her new-found clarity and anger toward the drunk-driver who killed her parents – what could I possibly say?

Chapter Twenty-One

McKenna

I couldn't wait any longer. After the four hour drive with nothing but the radio to keep me company, I couldn't resist going straight to Knox's place. With darkness settling in, I parked on the street and grabbed my overnight bag from the backseat before jogging to the front door. I'd been planning on coming home tomorrow, but as the morning had stretched on, I became more and more anxious to see Knox. I'd hastily packed, said my goodbyes, and hit the road. I wanted to surprise him.

Tucker answered the door a few moments later.

'Kenna!' He latched himself around me, squeezing tightly.

'Hi, bud. I missed you.' I leaned in and kissed his forehead.

'I missed you, too. Are you back for good?'

'Yep. I sure am.' Following him inside, the cozy familiar feeling of being home settled over me. A tower of Legos was half-built on the living room rug and the TV was playing cartoons. The house even smelled the same. I inhaled deeply, breathing in the scent of boys. 'Where is everyone?'

'Luke and Jaxon went out somewhere, but Knox is here.'

My heart picked up speed. I couldn't wait to see his deep soulful eyes, to kiss his scruffy jaw, inhale his masculine scent. I'd missed him so much. 'Where is he?'

'Knox?' Tucker asked.

I nodded.

'He told me to wait down here. He brought a girl upstairs.'

My stomach dropped like a stone and I broke out in a cold sweat.

'McKenna? Are you okay?'

I pulled in a lungful of air. 'I'm fine.' I couldn't let him see the blood rising in my cheeks or the sheer panic in my eyes. Turning from Tucker, I marched up the stairs. The journey up the three flights of stairs felt like an out of body experience. I floated above myself and watched my legs climb each step, my shaky fingers gripping the banister. My pulse thundered in my ears as I waited outside his closed bedroom door. With my heart pounding way too rapidly to be safe, I raised my fist to knock. Then stopped. And listened.

Low feminine moaning followed by Knox's voice giving some type of command.

Bile shot up my throat and I swallowed, forcing the sickness down. With tears clouding my vision, I reached for the door knob and pushed open the door.

What I found inside the room was the last thing I'd expected to see. I fell to the floor, my legs giving out beneath me as the adrenaline in my bloodstream rioted.

'McKenna?' Knox's confused voice asked in the distance.

The moaning hadn't stopped and I brought my hands up to cover my ears and squeezed my eyes closed. Footsteps crossed the room toward me and I felt Knox's strong arms close around me, and movement as he lifted me from the floor.

'Breathe, angel,' he whispered into my hair. 'Amanda, clear a spot on the bed….' I felt him place me on his bed and I began to thrash, trying to sit up, to move but his hands held me firmly. 'Stay put. We need to talk.' His low authoritative voice whispering my name was the last thing I heard before I let the blackness pull me under.

www.ingramcontent.com/pod-product-compliance
Ingram Content Group UK Ltd.
Pitfield, Milton Keynes, MK11 3LW, UK
UKHW022259180325
456436UK00003B/149

9 780008 133962